THE GIRL IN THE GARDEN

The Girl
in the
Garden

Melanie Wallace

Houghton Mifflin Harcourt

BOSTON   NEW YORK   2017

Copyright © 2017 by Melanie Wallace

For information about permission to reproduce selections from
this book, write to trade.permissions@hmhco.com or to
Permissions, Houghton Mifflin Harcourt Publishing Company,
3 Park Avenue, 19th Floor, New York, New York 10016.

www.hmhco.com

Library of Congress Cataloging-in-Publication Data
Names: Wallace, Melanie, date.
Title: The girl in the garden / Melanie Wallace.
Description: Boston : Houghton Mifflin Harcourt, 2017.
Identifiers: LCCN 2015043036 (print) | LCCN 2016002054 (ebook) |
ISBN 9780544784666 (hardback) | ISBN 9780544784208 (ebook)
Subjects: LCSH: Unmarried mothers—Fiction. | Mothers and sons—
Fiction. | Family secrets—Fiction. | New England—Fiction. |
Psychological fiction. | BISAC: FICTION / Literary. | FICTION /
General. | FICTION / War & Military.
Classification: LCC PS3573.A42684 G57 2016 (print) |
LCC PS3573.A42684 (ebook) | DDC 813/.54—dc23
LC record available at http://lccn.loc.gov/2015043036

Book design by Kelly Dubeau Smydra

Printed in the United States of America
DOC 10 9 8 7 6 5 4 3 2 1

For Peter

1974

Mabel

MABEL KNEW BEFORE the girl came to speak with her what she'd say: that the man who hadn't so much as posed as the girl's husband hadn't returned and wasn't going to. She—Mabel—had surmised—no, she later told Iris over the phone, correcting herself, *not surmised but known*—from the moment she first saw them that he'd already washed his hands of her. For when he got out of the car he disregarded the girl, left her to open the passenger-side door and manage to get to her feet, stand, with that sleeping infant in her arms. He didn't even glance behind him to check on her, just walked toward the office porch and left her to trail him.

Midweek, afternoon, off-season. The autumn air was damp, still, the sky undulate with silken cirrus under which Mabel had been hanging sheets on the lines between the office and the last of the cabins. Two of those were occupied, four yet to be cleaned and shuttered, three still ready for any comers. *Any,* Mabel told herself, but she was nothing if not discerning about whom to rent to and whom to turn away, she'd had years of trial and error; and if the girl hadn't had that baby in her arms despite not looking much older than a child herself, Mabel would have said *Sorry, I'm closing up for the season*. But there she was, trailing him as though shy of him as Mabel approached, wiping her hands on the bleach-stained smock she was wearing over her sweater and jeans. Good day, she greeted them, which made the girl stop and examine the ground at her feet as he responded by giving a nod in the direction of the office and saying, I take it that vacancy sign is good.

He followed Mabel in, the screendoor closing behind him so that the girl had to let herself through it. She didn't stand next to him but behind and off to one side, head bent over her child. Mabel took in her stooped posture, the bluish half-moons under her eyes, the flush that rose to her cheeks when he told Mabel that he expected she might lower the price of a cabin if they stayed a while. How long's a while? Mabel asked. Ten days, he replied, which made the girl look sharply at him, then glance away quickly and hunch even lower over the cache in her arms, Mabel catching in the girl's expression what she thought might be consternation or dismay—or, she later considered, fear, as if the girl thought he had eyes in the back of his head and would be able to see her consternation or dismay or fear, shielding herself from what Mabel already realized the girl could not. At that instant, she—Mabel—knew she would not, for the girl's sake, refuse them a cabin or a lower price, and so gave them both.

He reached into a front pocket and peeled off from a roll of bills the cash he placed on the counter, the girl now watching slantwise and in amazement because, Mabel figured, she hadn't known he'd had that roll on him or hadn't ever seen that much money, or both. Mabel said the keys would be to the cabin called Spindrift—each cabin had a wooden sign with its name carved into it, hanging above the doorframe—and added that it was the furthermost from the road and the quietest, so nothing should disturb them there. He sleeps good, the girl murmured then, shifting her weight from one foot to the other and looking at the man beseechingly as if, Mabel later told Iris, giving him the chance to admit the infant not only existed but wasn't any bother. He turned and glared speechlessly at the girl for a moment, returned to glare at Mabel, his eyes as bloodshot and dry and glassy as Mabel's husband's used to be after driving the rig with Jimmy Devine, hauling loads around the country for weeks on coffee and bennies and willful stubbornness and the occasional catnap taken in the bunk he and Devine had built into the cab to allow one of them to sleep while the other was behind the wheel. Mabel took in that glare and watched him work at blinking it away. She recognized exhaustion when she saw it, and she knew by those eyes, by the way his unwashed clothes hung on him and the way he smelled, that he'd been driving day and night, night and day, and that he'd simply given out on her doorstep. *My luck* were the words that went through Mabel's mind just then: it was only happenstance that they'd ended up at the cabins, that he'd come to the point of needing a good deal of rest before he could get behind the wheel of that dusty, dented old Buick and face a round of endless driving once again. It went without saying, to Mabel's way of thinking, that when the time came and he was ready, he aimed to drive off alone.

So, we're square, he said, nodding at the cash on the counter, putting his hand out for the keys. We are, Mabel returned, but I'll need some ID for my records and your receipt. I don't need—he began to protest, but Mabel cut him off with: It's the way I do business, on the level. He eyed the bills she hadn't touched, and Mabel told Iris later that if he hadn't looked like he'd fall over from exhaustion any minute, he would probably have just scooped up what he'd put down and told her to go to hell. Instead, he turned on his heel and pushed past the girl, letting the screendoor slam behind him. That woke the infant, the girl saying Oh I'm sorry as the baby burst into whine and cry, then slipping away, letting the door shut gently behind her and standing on the porch rocking and cooing at the infant, her thinness so silhouetted by the screendoor through which Mabel gazed that she found it distressing. As disturbing was the way the man spoke to her when he approached, then watched her do as he said and waited for her to make her way over to the Buick and slide herself in.

The license he handed Mabel was from a Far West state. He was at least three inches taller than the height stated on it, and his eyes weren't hazel. Mabel wrote the name on the license into her registration book and filled out a receipt, telling him as she did what he needed to know. That the stove was electric. That the refrigerator was on. That there was a new showerhead, extra blankets in the closet. Not to use the towels for the beach. That they were responsible for making up the cabin — if they chose to make it up at all. On their fifth day, she'd bring them fresh towels and sheets and collect the used ones. The television got two channels clearly, a few more if you played around with the rabbit ears. The public telephone was located on the outside of the office to their right. Roland was the night manager, the office closed at 11 P.M.; she, Mabel, reopened it at eight in the morning. There were directions in the cabin to nearby grocery shopping and beachgoing. And she knew he wasn't even half listening, standing there in a lank way and breaking out in a filmy sweat, vacantly watching her handle that license. When she handed it back to him with a receipt and the keys, she asked if he wanted a crib. Crib? he repeated. For the baby, she said. Nah, came his response.

Well, if you change your mind —

I won't, he told her. And left abruptly, again letting the screendoor slam, the violence in his stride so visible that the girl hurriedly swung her legs — she'd been sitting with the passenger door open, her feet resting on the ground — into the car and shut the door before he could reach her. For he wasn't the type, Mabel knew, to open or hold or close a door for that girl, and that wasn't because he'd gone with no or too little sleep while putting towns, cities, counties, states, most likely an entire continent between where they began from and where Mabel was standing. Knew, too, that he wouldn't come back into the office to ask for anything, and certainly not that crib, which was something the girl and infant had most likely so far done without anyway. And knew, too, that he'd keep that girl cowed on a tight rein, because nothing was going to change, at least not on his watch during this stopover; and even if he didn't consider himself as being on watch, this was the way Mabel saw it.

And maybe she was right and maybe she was wrong, Roland chided her, standing with one foot crossed over the other and leaning an elbow on the office counter, having listened to Mabel recount their arrival that afternoon and her premonitions. The scent of low tide, beached seaweed, salt damp, exuded from his clothes, his skin; that Roland wore the aroma of the shores he walked, rain or shine, snow or sleet, every afternoon before arriving punctually at five — as he had for two years, more now, since a few weeks after her husband's funeral — never failed to impress her. Arriving just — as Roland put it in the beginning—because he was around, not asking Mabel whether she needed or wanted help and at times ignoring her altogether if she stayed on in the office rather than retreating upstairs to the apartment she couldn't bear because Paul was in the ground and would never return, would never again need her or their home or those shirts, pants, jeans, sweaters, jackets, caps that were still in his closet, his underclothes and socks still in the left-hand dresser drawers, his razorblades and shaving soap and aftershave in the medicine cabinet: all she had left of him. Between Paul's summer funeral and the November day she hung out the closed for the season sign, she grew accustomed to Roland's imperturbable constancy, although what had actually brought him around she never questioned—she was too numb—and he never mentioned. Though they'd never before been friends, they were locals and so not strangers to each other; he'd been two years behind her, had disappeared to state college the year Mabel married Paul, and four years later had returned with a degree and taken a position teaching in the high school they'd graduated from. Just helping out, Roland eventually announced, coming by daily and not acting as though nothing had happened but not asking questions, never insinuating that she should talk about losing Paul, about her grief. And he wasn't chary of her. He remained at ease and self-contained and, by the following season after Mabel opened, took over the care of those issues that sometimes arose in the night, chasing off raccoons that hankered to tip over garbage cans, quieting cabin dwellers partying too loudly, determining whether drunken kids who could barely stand never mind drive should be escorted into a cabin. He became the lifeline that saved Mabel during the most desolate winter of her life, between closing and opening the year she lost Paul, Roland continuing to pass by often and for no reason at all but for the fact, he reminded her, that her place was a natural stopover on his way between beachcombing and the night.

Roland's chiding did not rankle her, for Mabel knew she was right. She trusted what Paul had always said was her sixth sense, and she'd looked this stranger straight in those eyes whose color did not match that recorded on the license he'd proffered and in them recognized a wariness that could not mask his dishonesty or wiles, never mind his resentment of having been hamstrung by a girl and baby. She'd looked at him hard and intuited what he was capable of, could imagine him grim with glee because someone had defied him to swing into a hairpin turn at an insane speed or because he'd just walked into a bar and seen his mark or because he'd come across a lone female stuck with a flat in the middle of the night and in the middle of nowhere, and, in changing her tire, got caught up in the thrall of having coolly reckoned her gullibility, his possibilities. Mabel caught more than a glimpse of the person behind those eyes, saw through a man who might do anything with a calculated lassitude and cold equanimity, certainly without shame, if he thought he could get away with it or had no other way out. And Mabel knew, she told Roland then (and later told Iris over the phone), that that girl and infant would have been at what little mercy that man had left, and that by renting them a cabin she had already given him the way out he was seeking. If she hadn't, he'd have found other lodging, and the result would be the same.

Nothing persuaded Mabel to reconsider her opinion, not Roland's chiding, and not the fact that during the following days the man didn't disappear. But Mabel's sense of what was to come wasn't dispelled by what she witnessed, for by the way the girl acted it was obvious to Mabel that she feared what Mabel already knew, that he was just biding his time. There was the way the girl placed a small, frayed baby blanket on the ground in front of the cabin each morning and played with the baby, the man eventually coming to stand in the open doorway and gazing off, never approaching or joining her, the girl receiving neither nod nor grunt in response to anything she said to him, instead being met with a malicious silence and withering gaze while he studied her and that infant as if trying to figure whether they were animal or mineral or vegetable before then looking off, indifferent to her again, not giving a damn for the answer. The way she always trailed him with the infant in her arms, whether to the car—always letting herself in on the passenger side as he revved the Buick's engine—or to the shore on foot, passing the office with her holding the baby and carrying a bag over her shoulder, him leading the way empty-handed and without a backward glance. The way she was downright afraid to speak with Mabel when she encountered her at the clothesline one morning, the girl—without the infant—having draped over a line the diapers and baby clothes she must have washed and rinsed by hand. Upon Mabel's approach, she threw a furtive glance in the direction of the cabin to check that he wasn't standing in that doorway, watching and weighing what the two of them might say. Mabel told Roland that even if she'd been blind she wouldn't have misunderstood the girl's fear: she wasn't to speak to Mabel or to anyone, and no matter how bad things were for the girl Mabel figured they'd worsen if she persisted in striking up a conversation. Which she didn't. Instead, she told the girl quietly as she passed her by, There are clothespins in that hanging bag, just help yourself, and went toward the far end of the clothesline to hang the wash she was carrying.

Mabel kept her distance and her back to her as the girl pinned the garments, heard her say her thanks quietly, sensed her move off in the direction of the cabin, and found herself peering from the corner of her eye to check whether he'd opened the door and seen that Mabel and the girl had come across each other.

He hadn't. But Mabel was right: he didn't want the girl to have anything to do with Mabel. For on the morning she approached the girl sitting on the ground by the infant she'd placed on that frayed baby blanket in front of the cabin, Mabel carrying a change of sheets and towels, the girl called out for him before Mabel got close. When he stepped out from the cabin, he said something that sent the girl to scooping up the infant and going back inside, him not acknowledging either her or the baby, just stonily eyeing Mabel's approach and then saying something over his shoulder that made the girl reappear, holding the sheets and towels they'd used. She passed him and met Mabel halfway, the look on her face beseeching Mabel to let the exchange take place with nothing more than a nod. As the girl retreated, Mabel called out to him, *Everything fine?* but he only cocked his head to the side in response.

And that was that: Mabel didn't have any reason to approach them again, just took note of them doing what they did every day, him standing framed in the cabin doorway apart from the girl and infant, watching the horizon with an expressionless disregard, the girl always close on his heels with the baby in her arms and letting herself into the car, them driving off and returning, them walking past the office and crossing the road to the dunes and beach with him in the lead and the girl carrying both the baby and bag. Until the morning he drove off alone, coming down the long drive slowly enough for the girl to walk alongside the Buick with her fingers on the handle of his door, him looking straight ahead until they reached the road's edge, where he stopped the car for a moment, the girl bending toward his open window until something he said made her straighten and take a step back. And then the car turned onto the road, and she watched it disappear, then stood there rocking the child for a long time before returning to the cabin. From whence she re-appeared with the baby in the late afternoon and walked back to the road, watching in the direction he'd gone and from which she must have expected him to reappear, standing there as long as she could without losing hope and then crossing the road, heading to where they'd always walked in single file and now bereft of him to follow. By the time she returned from the beach, the dunes, and made her way back to the cabin, Roland was in the office. Mabel nodded in the girl's direction and pronounced, So it's happened: he's gone for good, just before the Buick pulled in. Now eat your words, Roland told her.

The man drove down the drive the next morning, the girl again walking alongside the car and again being left behind. This time he didn't return, and late that afternoon Roland and Mabel watched the girl stand on the edge of the road by the drive until the dusk deepened with day's end. She walked by them in the gloom, Roland raising a hand to Mabel to stop her from going to the girl. If she needs anything, he said, she'll come by. But she didn't, not that evening and not the next day or the day after that, instead just played with the baby in front of the cabin during the mornings and from time to time stood waiting at the roadside, and late each afternoon carried the baby across to the dunes and the shore, Roland still assuring Mabel that it was only a matter of time before the man returned, dumb-founding Mabel with his matter-of-fact refusal to break faith

with what Mabel considered to be his illusions regarding human nature. Mabel didn't argue, just waited out the time it took
for the girl to come to the only conclusion she could draw. That
came three days after the girl and the man who'd abandoned
her had overstayed their ten days. The girl came in through
the office door with the baby toward late afternoon, before Roland arrived, to tell Mabel what she later recounted to Iris she'd
known from the start. Ma'am, the girl said with as much dignity and composure as she could muster, he hasn't returned and
isn't likely to.

It's just as well, Mabel told her. Then watched as the girl collapsed into a chair and bent over her baby and wept—for the
first time in many years—into her hands.

She said her name was June. As though, it struck Mabel, she'd
never had or no longer had a last name or a need for one. She
told me she had forty-seven dollars and change on her, Mabel
recounted to Iris later over the phone, and I wasn't about to send
her on her way with that, not that she had anywhere to go. Nor
was Mabel about to discuss the girl's future, as her present was
disastrous enough, the thought of it almost intolerable. The girl
took a long while to cry herself out, and Mabel left her to do so
alone, leaving the office and walking to where the girl used to
stand at the edge of the road. The season was losing its warmth,
the air already tasted of deep autumn, and Mabel stood there
until Roland's VW Beetle came into view and she flagged him
down. He didn't pull into the drive, just braked and idled the
car and waited for her to cross the road, rolled down the window and upon seeing her expression said Oh no, to which she
replied Oh yes. All right, then, he told her, I'll be back. Mabel

nodded, suddenly aware that Roland knew that she would see the girl through, even if she hadn't fully considered the complications. And then he was gone, the VW's odd clacking purr still audible after the car was out of sight, Mabel listening until hearing nothing, seeing nothing but the empty road, and thinking *I'm now standing in her shoes, what if Roland never returns,* then perishing the thought but not quickly enough; she'd already felt that anvil of anguish lodge in her chest—abandonment has its own valence—and then she was telling herself *I'm being ridiculous, crazy, ridiculously crazy* and walking back to the office through the paltry, thin light that promised nothing more than a leaden dusk.

The girl was still in the chair. Mabel didn't try to comfort her because she didn't have the words; she'd never known what it was to have a broken heart at that age and like this, but she knew a great deal about loss and knew that the sorrow it spawns is impervious to consolation, allows no solace; Mabel had seen those thin shoulders heave, those thin hands wipe at the tears, and she'd heard that end-of-the-world sobbing and realized that the child—I actually saw her as a child then, Mabel later told Iris, I was suddenly terrified she might be no more than thirteen—had just come up against the hard irrefutable fact that he was gone. Mabel couldn't imagine what the girl had been through during those last few days, alone and wanting desperately to believe in him, clinging to the empty hope that he'd return, before finally losing the will to wait, believe, hope, which loss had most likely happened two minutes before the girl walked into Mabel's office and fell apart. At any rate, they stayed like that, the girl sitting crouched over her infant and crying until she finally fell into the silence Mabel refused to sunder, until Roland returned and, after leaving two bags of groceries at the door of the cabin that was now solely the girl's, came into the office and said hello and leaned against the counter, hooking his elbows behind him and resting them on its surface, telling the girl that he'd just dropped off some things and that she should let him know if there was anything else she or the baby might need, how beautiful the way the baby just slept on, what's his name? And through those glazed, cried-out eyes, the girl stared at Roland with the exhausted incredulity of someone falling endlessly through space, then finally found her tongue and managed: Luke, his name's Luke. Well, Roland said, we'll see to it that Luke is properly set up. And with that, he went into the back of the office and returned with a folding crib and mattress and passed through its silence, let himself out, headed back to the girl's cabin. He'll set it up, Mabel said, and June swallowed hard, shook her head slowly. I can't stay here, she said, I can't even pay you what I already owe. And Mabel realized the girl had crossed a line with that solitary *I,* that the reality of being on her own had sunk in.

Forget that, came Mabel's rejoinder.

But the girl forgot nothing; she came into the office early the next morning with the infant on her hip and looking as though she hadn't had a full night's sleep or any sleep at all, for despite the fact that her face shined from having been scrubbed, her eyes were swollen, and those blue half-circles beneath them had darkened. She'd pulled her wet hair back into a braid and wore a shirt that was twice too large for her thin frame; his, Mabel realized, realized too that he would have left behind what he wasn't wearing when he drove off as if that could have assured June—which it hadn't—that he'd return. At any rate the girl, in that ridiculously huge shirt, placed forty-seven dollars and change on the counter and said: Take this, and please let me work off what else I owe.

Mabel told her to keep the money, then told her what needed doing.

So, Mabel recounted to Iris, June stayed on. Doing more than what little Mabel could think to ask of her—at this time of year she didn't need help, she was able to cope with having a cabin or two rented out during the week and a few more on weekends—with a seriousness of purpose and with an inner reserve that, Mabel came to conclude, sprang from a combination of embarrassment, a well-guarded and self-protective sense of privacy, and a rather fierce determination to set things right by staying as busy as possible so as not to think. She swept and dusted and aired out the unused cabins daily, washed down refrigerator interiors and windows, scrubbed stovetops, set blankets outside to air, helped Mabel with the washing, hanging, folding of sheets and towels. She never spoke about the man who had deserted her, did not speak of her predicament or her past and, at least in Mabel's presence, never again broke down over the hand fate had dealt her. But Mabel would glimpse her carrying the infant and passing by at the break of day, cutting through the autumnal morning fog that rose like an exhalation from the warm ground, wisping phantasmagorical shapes in her wake as she and the infant moved as one being, solitary and silent, to disappear beyond the road and the dunes, returning only after the sun and breeze dispersed the miasma, revealed again the earth. June's diurnal predawn passage reminded Mabel of how she too, for months after Paul's death, had solemnly trespassed the threshold of each day and walked through the dunes, along the shore, staring at the water's immense and often indistinguishable horizon, given the half-light, the mist, wondering how she might survive her bereavement, that eternity of emptiness that had settled within her and stretched before her, and never finding a clue, just coming back answerless and slipping into the office before it was time to open, then getting through the daylight hours doing by rote what needed to be done and spending the nights curled in a chair, unable to sleep, unwilling to dream, incapable of feeling anything because grief so drained her, numbed her, hollowed her out, that she saw herself as no more than a shell whose once-living internal flesh was now desiccate. Mabel wonders how June survives the nights. Whether she finds the loneliness unbearable, whether she even manages to sleep: Mabel doesn't ask, June never mentions. But watching the girl drift each morning through the mist and return with the sun, Mabel reminds herself that at least she, Mabel, has had a life, married the man she loved and was loved in return, lived with him where she grew up, in this house among these cabins, except for those times — which could stretch into weeks, into months — he wasn't with her because of driving with Jimmy Devine.

The call of the road: Mabel never knew why it meant what it did to Paul. Babe, he'd tell her, think of the money, it covers us for wintering in Florida from January through mud season: think of that. But he didn't live for the winters they spent in Florida: hitting the highways with Devine had something to do with money but certainly less about their being snowbirds a few months each year than about the fact that Paul loved the going, the wildness of what he called roving, the stopovers for showers at truck depots, the characters sitting at as well as waiting upon diner counters, the way hookers worked their way from cab to cab in off-highway rest stops lightyears distant from any

city or town, the way the plains seemed endless, the way storms
could blow apart trailer homes being hauled or rain down hail-
stones the size of golf balls, the way lightning could erupt from
the earth and reach into the sky as well as vice versa, the way
he and Devine sometimes left the highway and took secondary
routes and stopped anywhere they pleased if the landscape, or
a hamlet that didn't deserve so much as a dot on the map, happened to awe them; the way there was always someone, mostly
kids and sometimes runaways, hitching a ride, needing to go
in any direction anyone who would pick them up happened to
be traveling in. The call of the road: Mabel didn't mind shar-
ing Paul with that, and she worked through the summers with
him gone much of the time, waited up nights in the hope that he
and Devine might pull over someplace that had a phone booth,
waited up to hear the operator's voice saying *Collect call for anybody from Paul, will you accept the charges* and then hearing his
voice, listening to him describe where they were, where they'd
been, the time they were making, the trouble with the rig, the
weather, someone they'd picked up, what they'd be hauling next
and to where: anything, Paul could tell her anything and nothing, just listening to him breathe was enough.

Would be even now.

And if June felt the same about the man who hadn't so much
as posed as her husband and was now gone for good? If she did?
How could she not? But no, Mabel insisted to herself, the girl
simply couldn't, she was too young, they couldn't have been together—if they'd ever been—an iota of the twenty-seven years
Mabel had had with Paul. And, too, there's the fact that the man
who left June wasn't dead, that June hadn't had to make her
peace with his demise; not that Mabel has made her peace with
Paul's death, but she's come to feel an unaccountable, inexplica-

ble familiarity with the notion of her own. She constantly considered killing herself after his funeral, every night for months she placed her bare feet in Paul's loafers to feel the shape of his feet, the imprint of his weight, recall the way he looked in the casket and try to feel the nothingness he'd become, indeed join him, so that every friend and acquaintance who made up the mourners at his funeral could no longer bother her with their casseroles and pies, cakes and homecooked meals she couldn't possibly eat, their heartfelt concern and pity. But she didn't die, couldn't kill herself, couldn't bear friends or pity, and stood in his shoes at night and wept and finally told their friends and acquaintances that she couldn't eat what they brought, didn't want company, that she needed time alone; if she couldn't be with her husband, she didn't want to be with anyone who would mention his name. Even now, she spurns proffered advice and resists any hint—from those friends who forgave Mabel her misery and came back into her life—of getting on in terms of finding someone else; Mabel has sworn there will be no starting over, she does not want to love or be loved by anyone but the man she has buried. June, Mabel thinks, cannot possibly feel what Mabel has: the girl can't have known that kind of love, maybe hasn't even ever been happy, and the man who's deserted her hasn't died, she hasn't had to see him dead or bury him: he's simply gone. So, Mabel reckons, no matter how crushed June is or how hard the going will surely be, she has the resiliency of youth and its forgiving forgetfulness on her side. More important, Roland quietly observed one evening, is that June has Luke to anchor her.

Mabel disagreed. Anchors weigh, she reminded him.

And moor, came his reply.

I'm not sure she sees it that way.

What she sees is an infant she loves. Who needs and loves

her in return. That's a given, a constant that won't change any-time soon.

If she didn't have that baby —

She'd be lost.

She already is.

No, Roland said, she isn't. She's here with us.

And he'd said that *with us* so naturally, without emphasis and without hesitation, that Mabel later reflected, for the first time, that Roland considered her a part of his life, that his stead-fast presence was as much about being a part of her life — as much as Mabel would allow — as it was about being himself. And maybe Roland *had* anchored her; not that she'd ever put it in so many words, but there he was with that waft of ocean wil-derness about him, again settling in for the evening and never mentioning his feelings, never asking anything of her, never seeming to mind whether she remained in the office or re-moved herself and went upstairs to stand in Paul's shoes or drop into the chair she still curled up in most nights. If she stayed in the office, he'd sometimes talk — Roland, easy with her si-lences, could hold a one-way conversation — about what he'd discovered or seen or done if he thought she'd be interested or just needed to hear him, anyone, speak about something other than the cabins, the rentals, the weather. He took in but never commented on how, in those first months following the mas-sive heart attack that stilled Paul's life, felled him instantly, the lines around Mabel's eyes and mouth had deepened, evidenced her sorrow, the tragedy of her loss. He hadn't dwelled on her bereavement or coddled her, just came and went and returned again, and she'd come to expect the sound of the VW pulling in or pulling out and to count on Roland's undemanding constancy without even knowing it, without knowing that he counted on her presence as well. When she put off closing the cabins the autumn after Paul died, Roland never asked when she intended to shutter them; he never mentioned the future, seemed oblivious of it, although of course he wasn't. Mabel has never been able to intuit the meaning of Roland's steadfastness because she has been and sometimes still feels herself to be so numb, distraught, lost, that to this day she doesn't know when she first noticed that Roland had rearranged what knickknacks, magazines, maps she had in the office and made room for the books he brought in on shore plants, crustaceans, marine mammals, waterfowl and migratory birds, seaweed, tides, meteorology, the constellations, edible wild plants, as well as the novels and collections of short stories he taught and those he might consider teaching at some time in the future. When she finally noticed—long after she'd given the cold shoulder to everyone but the strangers who stayed in the cabins—she repeatedly told him that he shouldn't have inconvenienced himself, didn't have to come by, drop in, hang around. I know that, he repeatedly countered.

June stayed shy of him. Perhaps, Mabel considered, would of men for some time to come; then again, June also stayed shy of Mabel, perhaps considering herself a burden but determined to be nothing of the sort, at any rate politely—always politely—refusing both Mabel's and Roland's offers to drive her into town when and if she needed anything, instead going on her own every few days, carrying Luke and that bag she'd used for the beach and walking the mile-and-a-half each way, returning with the child in her arms and the bag bumping up against her packed with what she'd bought out of that forty-seven dollars and change she'd been left with, and later the weekly pocket money — Mabel's words — Mabel insisted June take for the work she did. June politely objected to accepting money from Mabel, pointing out — also politely — that she couldn't, hadn't, paid for the cabin, but Mabel pshawed her: June wasn't keeping Mabel from renting out the cabin at this time of year, no one was banging on the office doors for a place to stay. Besides, Mabel informed her gently, you and Luke are going to need warm clothes for what's coming: winter's around the corner.

And of course June had noticed — who wouldn't have; the days were shorter, frost sometimes crusted the ground at night, the only fog now appeared at sea. The ocean's hue had gone from gray to cobalt, the sun no longer dried and bleached the sands beneath the hightide lines, and the bonewhite dunes of summer were blonder now, the shadows spilling beneath their crests a dull russet. The green of the conifers had deepened and lost luster; the birch and maple trees, sumacs and scrub oaks, willows and ailanthus had turned colors that would not be seen again until their buds bloomed in spring. June one day asked Mabel the names of those trees that had lost most of their leaves, which made Mabel realize June had never experienced the Northeast before, and because Mabel had no idea where the girl was from, she — without prying — took that opportunity to ask. June paused before coming up with a perfectly oblique answer. From a nowhere place, June told her, adding: You wouldn't know it.

A nowhere place, Roland later mused, doesn't strike me as somewhere she can return.

He didn't ask Mabel when she would close for the season, didn't ask her intentions, but knew the day was fast approaching when June and Luke would have to leave that unheated cabin. He waited for Mabel to mention the inevitable, but she didn't, despite the bite of the winds, the shifting shape of the dunes and shoreline, the heavy swells of low, rolling cloudcover keeping the sun at bay. The vacancy sign remained and the cabins went empty, and Mabel did not tell Roland what he already knew: that she could not bring herself to take June and Luke into her home, shelter the two through the winter, because even after two years she couldn't live with anyone but the man she'd buried, couldn't make room for or stand the nightly presence of anyone in the upstairs apartment but Paul, never mind a girl she barely knew and a baby she was growing fond of who would only remind her of what she and Paul had always wanted but never had. And maybe, Roland considered, she judged herself harshly for not taking them in, but he knew she was not ready to allow herself the privilege of being needed, never mind loved again—even by a girl or a child—without feeling, no, knowing, that this would eat away at her loss, consume her mourning, disallow her to constantly think of and remember Paul, whose scent and voice had been lost to her, and whose face and body were now terrifyingly indistinct to her. Mabel wasn't ready to betray the one constant she stubbornly clung to: her past.

I can't keep them here much longer, Mabel finally tells Iris over the phone. Iris doesn't ask why Mabel won't bring them into her home: like Roland, she knows Mabel's reasons, and Iris doesn't consider them sane or insane, justifiable or indefensible: the two women have, to the extent each has been able, shared with each other certain confidences regarding their private lives, and Iris neither judges Mabel nor prompts her to continue; indeed, Iris doesn't say a word, and Mabel listens to the silence on the other end of the line. When she finally takes a deep breath and begins, Mabel doesn't insist, as Iris knew she wouldn't, *You owe me, I need this favor,* but both of them understand it's finally come to this.

Please take them in, just for the winter, Mabel says.

Well, Iris eventually responds, I'll have to send Duncan. Just, she adds lamely, to see if she'll suit.

I thought you might, Mabel replied in relief.

Duncan

THE GIRL WAS nothing like Claire, but of course Duncan could not help thinking of Claire as he drove back from Mabel's, where, on the pretext of interviewing June, he'd simply made sure that the girl didn't look like Iris's daughter and wasn't in temperament or character the way Claire had been at June's age, or ever. Why Iris would agree to take the girl and her baby in—if, in Iris's words to him, the girl would suit—was, to him, a mystery. Especially as Iris would house them in the cottage on her property, which cottage—so far as Duncan knew—no one had ever stayed or lived in except Claire, who had claimed it for her own at fourteen. No, he corrects himself, thirteen. Only thirteen then, and already unnervingly self-sufficient, determinedly on her own and simply undismayed by Iris, who was unwilling to have anything to do with anyone, including her own daughter, who hadn't minded at all—indeed, Claire had been the one to decide that she was perfectly capable of taking care of herself. She also hadn't minded that she'd been entrusted to Duncan, whom Iris had chosen to be her lawyer and, by extension, Claire's. If Duncan had been amazed by his first client, who happened to be Iris and who'd selected him precisely because he was new to town—which meant he had no connections with anyone in Iris's life, and no past in terms of the area—he also was shocked by the size of the monetary estate she placed in his hands. And shortly thereafter by Claire, whose nonchalance at being left to her own devices to get through life simply astonished him.

Claire relished the freedom of bringing herself up; she'd moved into that cottage of her own accord and acted as though every other thirteen-year-old did exactly what she was doing, living without parental guidance of any sort, and as though it were entirely reasonable that she should fend for herself. If Claire had any misgivings—which she never appeared to have—she never said. And if she mentioned her mother, Claire always did so succinctly, matter-of-factly, and always referred to her as *Iris;* and although she never spoke about Iris ruefully or resentfully, neither did she speak of her with any fondness. Claire was—and so far as Duncan knew, remained—in this regard and most other ways, profoundly circumspect.

She'd floored Duncan by the way she was able to take everything in stride, including him. If she'd ever been shy, she wasn't at thirteen or thereafter; and if she'd ever had childish interests, she no longer did by the time she became his ward—Claire's word, which she pronounced upon their first meeting without a hint of irony, just smiled as she spoke it before explaining that, burdensome as he might find certain responsibilities, Iris couldn't and wouldn't attend parent-teacher meetings, arrange for appointments with—never mind accompany her to—a doctor or dentist, write notes that would excuse her from school if she was sick, or evince the slightest interest in the grades she, Claire, would receive. And so, Claire had continued, these duties would fall upon Duncan's shoulders, but she wasn't clear as to what paperwork Iris needed to sign to allow him to stand in Iris's stead, and Iris certainly wasn't going to ask. Duncan, confronted by the sight of this small, dark-eyed, very slight eighth-grader who could have passed for an elf dressed in overalls and sneakers, did his best to show nothing of his astonishment at what she had to say and the way she spoke to him, as though she were his equal in age and had known him all her life, and as though this situation accorded perfectly with the natural order of things. He told her that Iris had directed him to draw up the necessary papers concerning his responsibilities in regard to Claire, and that he was in the process of doing so. Claire thanked him for taking into account her concerns, shook his hand, took her leave, and left him wondering how any child could be as reasonable, confident, and self-effacing as this one.

He'd never come up with an answer. Couldn't even now.

No: June wouldn't remind Iris of Claire. But surely her mere presence would disturb. Not that this would be his problem; Duncan had to take Iris at her word, even though he suspected that something he couldn't fathom was behind her decision to shelter a perfect stranger, one with a baby, at Mabel's request. Iris told him only that she could use a bit of help—which he couldn't refute, although it was the first he'd heard of such a thing—and, of course, it made perfect sense to him that, if she indeed needed help, Iris would rather have a stranger from nowhere than anyone from town. For, without ever saying as much, as far as Iris was concerned no one from town, actually no one from within a fifty-mile radius, could be expected not to spread the word that he or she had actually come face to face with Iris. Duncan knew Iris wasn't wrong; after all, she'd held herself aloof, remained a recluse for so long now that rather than being forgotten she'd become legendary, both because of her withdrawal from the town and because of the outrageous circumstances of her husband's death. Immediately following his demise and the beginning of her self-imposed isolation, Iris was forgiven, but later—when it became apparent she was going to continue shunning any and all contact with the outside world, at least so far as anyone and everyone knew—she was resented.

Except, of course, by Claire. Who, vacationing with Iris at Mabel's, had been left behind by her mother of a Saturday morning when her father did not appear as expected and couldn't be reached by phone. Iris borrowed Mabel's car and drove back to her home alone, only to discover his body. Iris didn't tell Claire that her father was dead, just told her there was a problem and that Claire was to remain with Mabel for the rest of that summer. Which she did, and then stayed on through that school year while, unbeknownst to Claire, Iris withdrew from local society and hired workers from elsewhere to erect a stockade—Claire's word—around the property's perimeter, then brought in carpenters and cabinetmakers (also from elsewhere) to gut and redo the house to Iris's satisfaction, most offensively (in the town's view) removing the windows and door that had looked onto the street and walling in the house's exterior on that side. Which was, Claire-at-the-age-of-thirteen later told Duncan—without a hint of criticism of her mother's decision to do so—the outward manifestation, a metaphor if you like, she elucidated, of Iris's resolve to turn her back on the world. Which, she added, I have to respect.

Respect: this again was the justification Claire gave Duncan when she announced that she was moving into the cottage to live on her own. You're *thirteen,* he'd protested. Well, she responded, her dark eyes holding his, the house I returned to isn't the house I grew up in: the kitchen and dining room aren't where they were, the appliances are all new, every piece of furniture was removed and, if replaced at all, substituted with Mission pieces; what had been my bedroom is now a sort of reading-and-sewing room, there are French doors that look onto the garden, floor-to-ceiling windows where there were walls, and walls where there were windows; there's a fireplace where there wasn't any, closets where there were none, no closets where they'd been, a pantry that never was, wainscoting with painted walls rather than wallpaper, and plank floors instead of linoleum. Iris has done everything she can to erase every trace of my father, of the life she had with him; even the sod's been stripped from what had been the lawn, the flower beds uprooted, and Iris probably intends to spend the rest of her life designing a garden of her sole creation. My presence in that house violates everything she's managed to do. After all, I'm their spawn—

Children are *not* spawn—

Spawn is most certainly the word Iris would use, Claire told him with a bemused look of pity.

I doubt that.

Duncan, she sighed, I'm the only person in the world Iris has to see, and she'd rather look at a goldfish. Believe me.

And he'd decided not to argue. Claire flustered him: he knew nothing about thirteen-year-old girls, and thirteen years had passed since he'd last been that age himself. He arranged some papers on his desk, gave himself a moment to think. Your grades better not suffer, he warned. Understood, she replied.

And then appeared at his office every Friday to collect her allowance, which sums she managed and, to his wonder because he'd never prompted her to do so, gave him an accounting at the end of each month as to what she spent and why. She never asked for more than what she received, and from those weekly payments saved and bought what she'd decided she most wanted: a professional's camera.

Duncan had thought about Claire obsessively those first few years after she'd left town. It took a long time for him to erase her from his mind upon waking, a longer time to adjust to the fact that she was not going to return. He eventually reconciled himself to that loss—yes, he considered her absence his loss—and eventually his regret diminished, although today, now, because of the interview with June, who bears no resemblance whatsoever to Iris's daughter, he's overwhelmed by nostalgia for that exacting way Claire looked and spoke, for her no-nonsense sureness of who she was and who everyone around her was. He has no idea of what Claire looks like anymore; time must have changed her outwardly, perhaps softened her body's compact angularity, perhaps faintly etched lines about her eyes and mouth, but he knows it would not have changed her within: Claire's determination to do precisely what she wanted or needed, a trait that kept him and everyone else—Oldman excepted—who came in contact with her off-balance and often taken aback, would not have slackened or softened. In the fourteen years since Claire left, there had been the occasional phone call—her voice the same, surprisingly deep for someone so physically slight, her tone even, as always, perfectly matter-of-fact—to inform him of a new bank account number or phone number and address, Claire never beginning the conversation with *Hello* but just saying his name as though it were a sentence. And then pausing, waiting for him to do whatever he had to, clear his throat, cover the mouthpiece and excuse himself if in the middle of a conversation with a client or, as more often happened, with someone who'd just dropped in to fill him in on what they'd seen or heard that day, maybe put an elbow on his desk and rest his forehead against the palm of his free hand to steady himself before greeting her with *Hello, Claire.* And then she'd convey whatever information she'd called about, and Duncan would tell her how the estate stood despite knowing that Claire wasn't interested in those details. She never asked after Iris, and he never mentioned her: he knew that Claire touched based annually with Iris somewhere around that occasion of out-with-the-old-and-in-with-the-new and that those calls had nothing to do with holiday wishes, for Iris spurned any interest in holidays and had celebrated none since her husband had died. What mother and daughter spoke of, Duncan couldn't begin to guess, but he suspected that Claire did not talk about herself and that Iris did not ask, that the *How are you?* on both sides was superficial and less important than discussing—curtly—the weather. Claire spared Duncan such small talk during her infrequent calls. But, after telling him whatever she needed to inform him of, and after listening to whatever he told her, she invariably ended with: *So, Duncan, are you spoken for yet.* She never inflects the question. He never answers truthfully *No*—for then she might come back—or *Yes*—for then she would never. He only ever answers, in a cautionary, admonishing tone, by saying her name.

Claire.

He hasn't spoken to her in more than a year now. He assumes Iris will not tell her about the girl during their more or less annual phone conversation. He will not call Claire: he doesn't. And, if she calls, he won't breathe a word about Iris's decision to take in the girl: it is not his place. Besides, Claire won't ask about Iris: she doesn't. And he hasn't mentioned Iris to Claire since the month after Claire moved herself into the cottage from the house in what she called Iris's compound and had become a fixture in his office, arriving unannounced almost daily to curl up in a corner armchair and do her homework, intent upon whatever it was she was reading or writing, not unmindful of but ignoring the fact that her presence made him uncomfortable because he still hadn't the slightest idea of how to deal with her. For she rearranged his senses, disquieting him, when she looked up and studied him from time to time with those liquid dark eyes, knowing he was already hiding behind his role of guardian because he couldn't be anything but and didn't trust her to be or act the age she was. In response, he'd sometimes ask how Iris was rather than inquire about school or whether Claire thought it was going to rain, any chitchatty question to which the answer wouldn't matter; and for a while Claire tolerated the question, always responding *Perhaps fine, perhaps not.* He hadn't exactly expected Claire to tell him that Iris had objected to Claire's move or at least noticed that Claire was living on her own, but the day came when Claire—in answer to his question as to how her mother was faring, that last, final time he ever asked—looked at him in mild exasperation, considered him the way a weary teacher might a rather dull but somewhat droll student, and remained silent. He shuffled a few papers on the desk in front of him and then stilled his hands and met her gaze, saying firmly: I asked how your mother is.

Cocooned, came her answer.

Meaning?

Meaning exactly that. She's wrapped around herself and

hanging by a thread. Which is the way she'll always be. I don't know why you insist on asking.

I'm normal, he told her peevishly. Normal people usually try to be polite by asking normal questions—

And make the mistake of thinking they'll get normal answers. You're asking about *Iris*. You can't seriously think I'd say, *Oh, she has a headache today* or *Fine, thank you, but really sorry she can't drop by, she's on her way to the hairdresser's* or *Really happy to have gone away last weekend and seen her old friends.* There isn't a platitude in a thousand that can be said about Iris.

Claire, you could have just said: *The same.*

Duncan, she responded, I'm not good with generalizations. They obscure specificity.

What?

The truth, Claire said. Which I assume might interest you, as a lawyer.

Well, as a person, I'm interested in niceties.

Well—Claire returned, perfectly mimicking his inflection—I don't have any use for them. Or for illusions.

And that, Duncan knew, was what had drawn her to photography: for, as she once told him, photographs aren't and can't be anything but what they are, a slice of truth captured in a split second, which truth has neither past nor future despite the questions it might raise about both. He drives along the coastal highway the old-timers call the old post road, a two-laner that's seen better days since the inland highway with its four lanes—a few years back, expanded to six—left this route mostly untraveled. He's always loved this drive north, hasn't taken it for years, but as he is giving himself over to his memories of Claire—not that he could stem that tide if he wanted—he finds himself gladdened that they've piqued his nostalgia for this route his grand-

parents always took to their summer rental with Duncan rid-
ing along in their plush sedan, which had mounted vases and
a braided silk rope strung across the back of the front seat. He
rolls down the window now, braces against the rush of cold, in-
hales deeply, recalls his thrill at the thought of every vacation in
that house on that cliff lasting an entire month, his grandparents always staying two weeks before his parents arrived, and
then the family remaining together for another two. It's the one
constancy from childhood he remembers, being in love with this
drive and those vacations and with the cursory visits to the town
beyond the summerhouse, which town he—or so it strikes him
now—chose to live in long before he ever had any knowledge of
his decision.

The tires *thump-thump* —as they did back then—across the
seams separating perfectly identical spans of concrete, and he
finds the sound soothing. He drives close to the center line to
avoid stretches of eaten-away shoulders, slows over frost heaves
and cracks and around potholes, follows meandering climbs
and dips that curve and spoon into the shape of the coast, drives
toward a horizon he will never reach. A silver strip illuminates
earth's end below the unbroken graphite sky. To his left, beyond the empty opposite lane, expanses of marsh and bog bordered by forests, and beyond the forests, he knows, clearings
of pastureland, the occasional horse or dairy farm, here and
there plowed fields still sown in late spring for corn and potatoes, old farmsteads lived on by those who'd inherited them and
kept to the ways of raising horses and cows and crops. To his
right, the ocean, spilling into rockstrewn coves, the occasional
sandy beach, glowering beyond the dunes and beneath cliffsides
topped by massive homes in which three generations, more, used
to live, homes with columns and wide porches, gables and wid-

ows' walks and cornices carved to reveal spandrels of leaping fish or shamrocks or anchors, their trim always painted a gleaming alabaster and their shingled walls invariably that blue-gray shade most often seen during winter's dusk, their zigzag access to the beaches below provided by weathered wooden staircases. The marshes, bogs, miniature estuaries, cliffs, coves, beaches, promontories and dunes go by in errant rotation; no one place is exactly like another but, then again, they all bear great resemblance to one another, with everything always ending or beginning at the edge of the ocean, beyond whose farthest rim, it occurs to him, lies England or France. It strikes Duncan, for no reason and suddenly, as queer that he has no idea of which latitude he is on.

Such specificity often escapes him. He can never remember exactly when Claire bought herself that first camera, but knows it was sometime before she graduated from eighth grade—which graduation he, not Iris, attended—and turned fourteen, for she was already being seen everywhere, biking in and outside of town, always alone, always with the camera. That summer she photographed every animal she espied until there wasn't a creature she hadn't, unless it was never let outside or never perched on a windowsill, and so captured on film every household pet and every horse, cow and anything else pastured within a ten-mile radius of her home, paying for the film and paying the local wedding photographer to make contact sheets as well as print what she chose, most likely spending, Duncan realized at one point, most of her allowance on what he considered a hobby and nothing on clothes. He finally brought himself to ask whether she was thinking of the dresses and skirts and blouses and sweaters she'd need for high school; Claire was changing shape before his eyes, and schools didn't allow girls to wear pants of any sort, never mind rolled-up boy jeans or overalls and oversize flannel shirts or T-shirts, which she lived in—those baggy, shapeless clothes of course actually drawing attention to the changeling she'd become, despite that ponytail. I'll worry about a wardrobe when the time comes, Claire told him, I'm busy right now putting the finishing touches on my first portfolio.

That portfolio sealed her fate, or at least the fate she'd already chosen for herself. And, Duncan considers now, not without relief, navigating the road's hug of the highest bluff of the coastline, determined his fate as well. For one photograph—of Oldman Smith's three capuchin monkeys romping through a meadow—was perfect: there was Oldman's pony, its coat and mane and forelock streaked with mud that had dried, making the creature look as if it had been carved in sandstone, leaning back into its bunched haunches that were up against a split-rail fence and looking as humanly spooked as any equine ever could, its taut neck vertical and its head horizontal, its front legs stiff with knees locked, eyeing those monkeys leapfrogging a bee-line toward it at some random speed. They were airborne in the photo, in a line, their long tails upright and long limbs stretched in flight above the knee-high grasses; and Claire, upon showing the photograph to Duncan, told him that that moment proved to her how feral—her word—beauty could be. She also told him that she had given a copy of the photograph to Oldman, along with portraits she'd taken of the pony and of his dog, which dog—Oldman later recounted to Duncan—he never thought anyone could get near without losing a body part never mind get the canine to pose, not to mention that the pony—whose headshot was taken from such a close range that he could count its eyelashes one by one—was expert at cow-kicking and had a way of snaking its head and chomping down on human flesh but had obviously, in Claire's case, done neither.

Oldman also told Duncan that when he saw that photograph of his escaped monkeys, he teared up. He claimed he wasn't a sentimental man, having seen and documented enough destruction and desolation and death while working as a photographer with the U.S. Army as it pushed into Germany and made its way to the Elbe to have persuaded, as he put it, the most solemn of believers that there wasn't much good in being sentimental; and Oldman was the first to admit that he hadn't started out as a believer in much of anything except chronicling what he saw. At any rate, nothing had so moved him since that first capuchin he'd raised like his own child—having bought and raised the baby monkey precisely because he was a bachelor and childless—turned on him one day and in a moment changed from a clinging and, as Oldman mistakenly believed, loving humanoid that seemed to understand even language but simply could not speak into the creature it was born to be. Who knows why, but most likely because the capuchin sensed in Oldman's manhood something that didn't sit well with its budding pubescence, the monkey Oldman had been holding—which had its arms around Oldman's neck, to the creature's advantage—leaned back, looked Oldman in the eye, and ripped open with its fangs Oldman's left eyebrow and, before he could throw the monkey off, filleted at a downward angle the rest of his face, tearing through the cartilage of his nose and ending in the vicinity of the right corner of his mouth. That left Oldman's right nostril hanging and blood flowing. The experience taught Oldman that monkeys make about the worst pets in the world, and after he had himself sewn up—he told Duncan that the local emergency room's receptionist actually fainted when Oldman came

through the door with his face split in half—he set about trying to understand why that was a fact. He built a spacious floor-
to-ceiling, two-compartment cage in what had been the storage
room located off his kitchen, which room had its own door with
a window that faced the side-yard garden in which Oldman
raised mutant pumpkins that one year grew large enough to re-
quire a forklift to move them onto and off the flatbed truck that
brought them to the annual pumpkin-growing contest at the
county fair. The cage had swings and deadwood branches and
a trap door between the two compartments that Oldman could
open and close so that, once lured into one or the other with
food, the capuchin could be contained while the other compart-
ment was cleaned. Oldman then set to reading about monkeys
in captivity, only to learn what he'd already been taught, that no
one could ever trust to get the wildness out of them.

And because, to Oldman's expanding knowledge, there
wasn't an animal farm or zoo in the nation that wanted yet another capuchin, Oldman realized there must be other fools—his
word—who'd bought a monkey for themselves or, worse, their
children, without an inkling of what was in store. He also decided to limit himself to a thirty-mile radius, then visited every
veterinarian within that to inquire whether they knew anyone
who had capuchins, and if so, could Oldman have their address.
Oldman's face was as convincing as anyone in their right mind
needed as evidence, which is how he came by two other capuchins, both female, one of which had already bitten a child and
the other of which had gotten into the habit of throwing its feces
at the household dog. So he came to own and truly care for the
three for a number of years, despite the fact that they sometimes
fought one another and always cannibalized the babies that
were born to one or the other female and occasionally latched

on to his hand or wrist with their prehensile tails as he was putting food into their trays, reminding him that they meant to
harm and disfigure whenever the opportunity presented itself
and that he should never mistake the intelligence in their eyes
for goodness.

One or two or all three of them finally figured out how to
undo the rather complicated latch on the cage's door, and when
Oldman went to check on them one summer morning they
were gone, escaped through the side-yard door Oldman frequently left open for the monkeys' viewing pleasure. Claire's
photograph was the last that he, or anyone, ever saw of them.
Still distraught at the thought of those creatures alone in and
maybe wreaking havoc upon the world, Oldman found himself wiping at the tears in his eyes in front of what he later described to Duncan as being the slip of a girl presenting him with
the photograph. Not because, as he told Duncan at some point,
the photo assuaged his fear that the monkeys would not be able
to fend for themselves, or wouldn't do damage to small animals
or children or anything else they took a fancy to harming, and
not because it consoled him to see the sheer joy with which they
seemed strung in midair as they flew toward his terrified pony,
and not even because he realized they were heading due south,
direction Latin America, as though they knew where their kind
came from. No, that photograph moved him to tears because
Oldman, in his own words, knew a work of art when he saw
one. Claire, he said, was also as sure of that photo as of herself; her maturity and seriousness simply rattled him as much as
that photograph and her portraits of other animals did. It didn't
take more than a long look at her work for Oldman to take her
under his wing, that same day bringing Claire and what she
called her first portfolio to the town newspaper, where Oldman

spent Friday and Saturday evenings developing film shot for its weekly wrap-up of community goings-on. He introduced her and her photographs to the paper's managing editor, who came to the not-unexpected decision to publish the capuchin/pony photo and write a piece to accompany it that included Oldman's advice as to what to do if the reader came across capuchins on the loose.

And that was that: Claire received a check for her first published photograph and signed it over to Duncan because she did not yet have her own bank account, and under Oldman's tutelage began going through his library, reading every photography book and every photographic journal he had, discussing theory and practice and the history of the art with Oldman, and spending Friday and Saturday evenings in the newspaper's darkroom at his side. Duncan had mused then, ruminates now, that Claire — better her than those capuchins — most definitely took the place of the child Oldman had never had, and that she became more a chip off the old block than any natural child of his perhaps would or could have been. Too, Oldman became the parent she didn't have, what with Iris, as Claire stated, cocooned, and her father dead. Whatever Oldman and Claire's relationship meant to Oldman and Claire, to Duncan's relief it meant that Claire — who not only didn't allow him to look upon her parentally, though he did, but also never set boundaries as to what their relationship might become — would not be ensconced in his office or life on Friday and Saturday evenings, and never on Sundays, which she reserved for experimenting with focal points, lighting, angles, and the different cameras and lenses Oldman lent her.

Relief, yes: he'd been relieved. For how impossible it had

been to not be troubled by her, to maintain his equilibrium; evenings after she'd left his office he'd often lock the door and collapse into his chair, trying to reassure himself that she hadn't the slightest notion of muddling his brain, rendering him insensate, but knowing otherwise: Claire grew perfectly conscious of her effect on him, amusedly relished his discomfort, and patiently waited for him to make the mistake he swore he'd never make. And he kept to his private oath, even when at June's age — sixteen — Claire announced at the beginning of the school year that Duncan was to take her out and dine with her on Thursday evenings at the Puritan on the town's main street. It's the night for going out, she told him, and I have no interest in being with anyone from school; I don't have girlfriends because my classmates, never mind the seniors, are obsessed to the exclusion of everything else in the world with finding boyfriends who'll want to marry after they graduate, perhaps even marry *them;* at any rate, they don't talk about anything but going steady and becoming engaged.

Well, as you don't have any girlfriends, find yourself a beau, Duncan reasoned, urged: I mean, for god's sake, date someone.

I'm not interested in dating, Duncan. I'm interested in going out and eating dinner at the Puritan on Thursday evenings, like everyone else does. And there isn't a person in town who doesn't know that you happen to be my mother's, and my, lawyer.

Maybe I'm spoken for on Thursdays after work.

Then bring her along, Claire replied, for god's sake.

And of course he wasn't spoken for then, not on Thursdays, and not on any other night. He told himself he didn't have any choice, asked himself what would be the harm. So that school year and the next, Claire's last, he locked up on Thursdays and accompanied her to the Puritan, where eyebrows were initially raised and a certain amount of chin-wagging took place, but as time went on no one paid them attention. And he grew used to their being together like that, with their heads bent toward each other, lost in those earnest conversations they held in low tones, Duncan ignoring or shrugging off looks from her that could not be mistaken in meaning; and when those dinners were over he always properly said good evening and saw to it that they properly went their separate ways. Claire—to his knowl-edge—never glanced back, just headed off into the night as he watched her slip in and out of the pooled streetlamp lightcones and make her way to the bus stop or to wherever she'd left her bicycle or sometimes just continue walking in the direction of her home, especially if the weather was rotten: she always said that inclement weather, rain and snow, sleet and wind, freed her mind from the mundane and let her live, as photography did, in the moment.

A moment's gone in an instant, he often cautioned her, you should be thinking of the future, considering college, deciding what you want to study. But Claire would have none of it; by sixteen she was interning at the newspaper, receiving a small salary, being given and always fulfilling photography assign-ments and working in the darkroom on Friday and Saturday evenings under Oldman's supervision, improving on what Old-man claimed was an already flawless professional portfolio, in-tending to work as a photographer, which, as she always pointed out to Duncan, demanded no college training and no degree, just a way of seeing and a will to go anywhere, anytime, to cover any situation or story. And of course Oldman had his con-tacts and used them. By May of her senior year, Claire had been hired, with a midsummer start date, as a photographer for a regional newspaper in one of the larger cities on the East Coast. Without Duncan's knowledge, Oldman had driven her—Claire had steadfastly refused to get a driver's license, although Duncan had glimpsed her behind the wheel of Oldman's old if sterling Studebaker from time to time—to and from her interview; twelve, fourteen hours' traveling time in total, Duncan calculated, as he sat across from her at the Puritan on a Tuesday afternoon.

For she'd appeared in his office at midday, the day after the interview he hadn't known about had occurred. The ponytail was gone, her dark curly hair cut within an inch of her scalp. Duncan intuited that this change—Claire was never frivolous, whatever she did was done purposefully—was ominous. She said: You need to take me to lunch. And he closed the office and they went to the Puritan, where eyebrows were raised once again, not only because her haircut was so radically different from what townspeople were accustomed to considering stylish but also because school was still in session. For the first time, he didn't give a damn what anyone thought: he was grappling with what Claire was telling him, that she'd had an interview and accepted a job offer, that she would leave town and become what she already was and had only ever wanted, intended, couldn't help be. That she needed him to write a note that excused her from school for yesterday and today.

He didn't ask whether Iris knew. He sat there, calculating the hours and distance Oldman had driven, before finally telling her his concerns: that she might not be able to handle the pressure, that there would be problems finding an apartment because of her age—although, as she pointed out, she would turn eighteen that summer and, as he knew all too well, upon that age would come into a great deal of money, none of which,

Claire told him, she intended to use except to set herself up; that Oldman had already made arrangements for her to stay in a women's residence for the first three months anyway—and that she'd never spent any time away from the town except when she'd lived with Mabel, that the world was a big and not always hospitable place. He sounded unconvincing, even to himself. They ordered chicken sandwiches and she ate hers slowly, heard him out until he finished cautioning her and found himself flustered because of the way she ate so deliberately, so delicately, looking at him evenly over that sandwich. She finally put what was left of it down and placed her arm on the table, leaned slightly forward, said: You could congratulate me.

Congratulations, he told her. The silence that ensued made him miserably self-conscious. He pushed away the plate he hadn't touched. You might not know what you're in for, he finally managed.

She nodded thoughtfully, as though considering he might be right, then half rose and leaned over the table, brushed his forehead with her lips, sat back. Duncan, she said, give me a reason to stay.

He felt himself freefall, came as close as he ever would at that instant.

I can't.

She held his eyes, finally cleared her throat, looked down at her plate, then back at him. Well, she finally pronounced, I just needed you to clarify that. For both of us.

Claire: Duncan almost says her name aloud, instead slows and pulls over onto the road's shoulder, stops and kills the engine, gets out of the car, walks away from it to the bluff's abrupt edge and examines the ocean below, its dark surface roiled, variegated, in the waning light. He has, for most of his life, thought dusk to be the most beautiful part of day; now he finds it the loneliest. Claire has stayed in constant touch with Oldman — not Duncan, not Iris — all these years: letters, postcards, long-distance phone calls, clippings, photographs. Duncan followed her career through Oldman, sometimes looked at an atlas to determine where she was or had been, finding the exact position of those foreign as well as Stateside places he couldn't quite locate in his mind, places he'd never been and would never go. And he'd come to a point in life — after the years it took for him to make peace with the realization she'd never return to the town he'd chosen to live in, convince himself that he could not have done anything other than he had, which was to remain righteous and never trespass the boundaries that being Claire's guardian placed upon him — where he realized that, despite the fact that as a lawyer he was more interested in truth than in honor, as a man he was more interested in honor than in truth. His behavior toward Claire — not his feelings — had been impeccable. It took time, but somewhere along the line he'd stopped being overwhelmed by how empty his soul was, by the crushing hollowness within whenever he thought of her and whenever Oldman told him what news he had of her. Duncan shakes his head, standing beyond his car, watching the sky and earth and waters go utterly dark. He has never been spoken for. So far as he knows, neither has Claire. He ruminates on his, her, their unspoken reserve: a mere coincidence, he persuades himself, and half believes the untruth.

Perhaps it's time, he considers as he heads back to his car, to think of allowing himself to be spoken for: there is Meredith to consider, that intelligent, companionable woman — quite new to his life — who hasn't pressed him to define their relationship or mentioned the future. He turns the engine over, switches on the headlights, drives on. He'll tell Iris that the girl will suit. He'd found June quiet, self-contained, because either shy or uncertain or both. Her answers to his questions were simple. She'd hesitated before speaking, seemed to carefully weigh her words, even when telling him her name, Luke's, her age, his. He's a good baby, she stated, the only thing she volunteered. She had a Social Security card, her birth certificate, Luke's birth certificate. She hadn't finished school. Duncan's question as to whether June was in any kind of trouble puzzled her; she'd furrowed her brow and looked at the baby on her lap quizzically before raising her eyes and meeting his, stating flatly: Well, there's the fact that I'm in this predicament. At which Duncan had smiled, clarified that he was asking whether she might be in trouble with the law, whether she was, say, a runaway, whether anyone might be searching for her. Oh no, came her response, I'm clean with the law, and no one in the world is looking for me.

He told her that she was welcome to stay in a cottage on Iris's property—he did not mention that it had been Claire's—and that the property was enclosed; that Iris, who lived in the house, might need help but Duncan couldn't say how much or what kind, and that June wasn't to bother Iris if Iris didn't let her know one way or the other. In that case, she should simply keep to herself, and would she be able to do that. The girl looked concerned, and Duncan mistook the reason for her expression, telling June that no matter what, June would receive a stipend. Her look of consternation gave way to confusion, and Mabel interjected that Duncan meant an allowance. On which you'll be able to live, Duncan added, which flummoxed the girl into stating that she didn't want to take charity or be a burden, that it was her intention—at which point Duncan interceded by raising a hand. You have to understand, he told her, that Iris is a recluse.

I don't know what that means, June said.

She lives alone, stays alone, and hasn't left her property for many, many years, Duncan replied. She doesn't have visitors, myself and Mabel excepted, and I see her only on those rare occasions when she needs to see me. Iris's only request, in terms of your staying there until next spring, is that you keep to yourself unless she tells you differently and that you come and go as you wish without bothering her.

But, why—

Iris is doing this because she can, Mabel said. And she'll have Duncan see to it that your only worry will be taking care of yourself and Luke.

I won't know how to thank her.

Just leaving her be, Duncan told her, would be thanks enough.

No, June didn't have any questions to ask Duncan, and didn't volunteer anything about herself. He tried his best to engage her, but the girl held herself close and who wouldn't. He can't imagine what she must be going through, having no more than a vague sense of where she'd ended up, somewhere alone in a state of which she had no knowledge except, probably, for the name she'd read crossing its line; at any rate, abandoned and penniless and with a child, at the mercy of strangers whose kindness—and Mabel was exceedingly kind—did not preclude, however, passing her on to yet another stranger. He didn't have the impression that the girl even understood her luck; indeed, to the contrary, she seemed broken by never having had any luck whatsoever. And he could only imagine that she'd come up hard in a hard place, although she wouldn't say with any specificity where that might have been, only quietly declaring she had nowhere and no one to go back to, and stating that without self-pity but with utter resignation.

She was flummoxed by Duncan's question as to what brought her to this part of the country. She looked so worried because of her own speechlessness that he realized she didn't understand he was trying to make small talk, and he was about to wave off any answer she might have been considering, which he figured had to have amounted to the story of her entire life, when she — after visibly struggling with her emotions — finally took a deep breath and ventured: I just always wanted to see the ocean.

June

WHEN SHE FINALLY found Ward and he'd taken her to the rooming house, he told her: Look, I'll see you through this and then you'll have to go, I'll take you anywhere you want, just name it. June was too stunned and too exhausted to reply, so he mistook her silence for indecision and said, There must be somewhere. And she still didn't reply, not because she didn't know the names of other places but because they meant nothing to her; she'd never been anywhere outside of where she'd grown up until now, or beyond where she was at that moment, sitting on the edge of the bed in Ward's annex room almost two hundred miles from where she'd left. She was seven months gone but hadn't known she was pregnant until the baby began moving around inside of her. That first pang so frightened her—she hadn't suspected, her breasts hadn't changed shape, her nipples hadn't darkened, she'd always had erratic periods—that she almost dropped to her knees, instead caught herself as she sank down, pulled herself up to where she'd been standing in front of the sink, steadied herself. She ran water over the glasses and plates and began to soap them when it happened again. The small sound she made was like that of a wounded cat.

It woke her mother. June heard her shift about on the couch, mutter under her breath. A clink of bottles, the flick of a lighter, the sound of a cigarette pack being crumpled. Fetid air turning acrid, and her mother's eyes on her back as June cleared out the sink. She took her time, trying not to panic at the alien thumps inside of her. It was late morning, the wind up and so strong it seemed visible, the blow pushing at the small window above the sink and rattling the trailer's siding, rippling the corrugated metal sheets that roofed Auntie's now-empty chicken coop across the way, lifting and snapping the roofing that strained against the bricks and stones weighing it down. Electric wires strung from listing poles whined and sang. One of the rotting trailers that had cantilevered off its cinderblock foundations rocked and groaned. It had once housed a number of feral cats whose eyes always ran pus and whose broods always sickened and died, but that was long ago, when the swing set's two swings still had seats instead of just chains holding nothing and dangling empty. That was when other people still lived in the trailer park that now sits isolate and rotting in an expanse of dented and desert-like land under empty skies. June barely remembers them. She doesn't know how many years it's been since the last of them, but for Auntie and her mother, left. Her mother never said how she came to be here or why she stayed on, and June never asked.

Not that she remembers her mother ever actually being here for any length of time, except for the summer a group of hippies came chugging down the long dirt drive from the road in a van that coughed and sputtered and gave out in front of one of the abandoned trailers, where they then camped for a few months. Their circus ways, their acrobatic antics, the way they danced and chased one another around and tumbled in and out of that trailer, their laughter, their wildly bright clothes when they wore any at all, their unashamed nudity, their drugs and drink kept her mother close until they pulled out that van's engine and, after a time, fixed it, then took her with them when they left. And that was the longest time June remembers her mother being gone. Why she came back, she never said. Never apologized for the going or evidenced surprise that June bothered to survive her absence. Never explained all those other times where she'd been or what she'd done on what she called her jaunts, never said where she got the black eye or split lip or wrist burns or jaw bruises, or where the men she sometimes brought back with her came from. Never inquired as to where June got the clothes on her back or if she brushed her teeth or who cut her hair or whether she'd bothered going to school or could read and write or count. Never said where the money came from for the booze and food and electricity, never mentioned the money she'd leave behind on the counter beside the sink just about every time she took to wandering off.

What's up with you, her mother says.

June wipes her hands, turns. If she's gone pale with whatever is probing her insides, her mother, slouched to one side on the couch, thighs half covered by a tattered afghan, doesn't notice or doesn't say. Rat-nest hair, ruinous eye makeup. The cigarette now drops into an overflowing ashtray by her feet, next to three liquor bottles, two of which are empty and another half gone.

Nothing, June answers. She walks over and picks up the ashtray, extinguishes the butt her mother dropped in. The smell of its burnt filter adds to the stench of the place emanating off the shag rug stained with spilled drinks and dust, the walls reeking of old varnish and damp and mold, the corners of the room stinking of bug spray, the uncovered pot of her mother's rank boiled cabbage and ham bone on the stovetop. Bring that back here, her mother says, reaching for one of the bottles and narrowing her eyes. June dumps the contents of the ashtray in the garbage pail, returns it to the floor by her mother's feet, picks up an empty bottle, barely avoids the kick that comes. Jesus, her mother says, stop it.

Stop what.

Stop fixing up things. This is *my* pigsty. Get outta my sight.

June lets the wind slam the door shut behind her, stands with her arms folded over her belly and rocks with the blow's ferocity, hair whipping at her face. Beyond Auntie's place, beyond the long drive, infinite flatlands whose sienna-blond surface is undulate with windsands. Sometimes, in the distance, dun-colored mustangs plod from horizon to horizon with their noses to the ground and tails slack, coming from and going to god only knows where through the detritus left behind by an ice age that had sculpted the world as far as the eye could see into an interminable and inhospitable moraine as barren as the moon. Sometimes, carrion birds float on the wing. Today there is only the wind and the shifting sands of that endless land beneath an empty sky, and the curious spasms within her.

Auntie, she says, entering the old woman's place.

I see she came dragging back under that slice of a moon, Auntie replies. How long you think she'll stay.

Well, she's got half a bottle. At least that's all I saw.

Huh. You cold?

It's worse out there.

I'm about to turn on the burners. Pull up a chair.

And she sits by the woman she knows only as Auntie, who is not June's or, to June's knowledge, anyone's aunt. The woman who, all these years, has taken her in. Has clothed and fed her and showed her how to clothe and feed herself—June learned how to sew and knit and cook before she could recall a time when she hadn't known—and seen to it that she sometimes went to school and admonished her never to cry just because the other children and the teachers shunned her, never to cry at all, for coming from this place there wasn't much more to expect than a shunning anyway, and not that that mattered. How old Auntie might be is a mystery to June, maybe to everyone in the town a mile-plus down the road, population 647, even to those two weathered old men who might or might not be Auntie's relatives and who arrive every so often, bouncing down the drive in that high cab of an old flatbed truck with their cache of bundled rags and bagged charcoal and grain sacks chock full of who-knows-what tethered to the backside. Of the rags, Auntie always takes her pick; she hooks rugs with those rags she doesn't use for sewing clothes, and she exchanges the rag rugs with the men for more rags, and sometimes even for cash. The cab doors stay open—folded horse blankets cover the seat springs—when they don't spend the night, and the doors are closed when they do, which is whenever they bring along a grouse or hen or fresh road kill, whatever they manage, for Auntie to stew. Who they are to her, who she is to the town, no one but Auntie knows, but one of the traders has more than once asked for what he calls a healing, a laying on of the old woman's hands.

June pulls a chair over, sits with her knees almost touching Auntie's. The old woman's lined face, profiled to the stove, shades from chamois fawn to mahogany. Her thick gray hair is pulled tightly back from her forehead and braided with colored strings. The windows are plastered with faded newsprint, and the light within the trailer hues golden, the two burners atop the stove glowing red. Auntie studies June's face with hooded eyes, eventually says: So you let her get your goat.

It's not that. It's not her.

So then.

I'm thinking I might need a laying on of hands.

Auntie cackles. Doesn't that beat all, she finally remarks, coming from you. And at your age.

June shrugs.

You got cramps?

Uh-uh.

Well then, what.

I don't know. It's like there's something inside me, pushing out. Plopping around.

Well then, stretch out on the floor on your back.

And June does, feeling the draft coming up through the floor's rotting underside, the cold on the small of her back and shoulders, the feel of Auntie's warm papery hands soft upon her barely tumescent tummy between her bare, bony hips. June closes her eyes, drifts beneath the old woman's quiet touch, those marvelous hands that had taught June how to sew and knit and crochet, those hands that might also, June reflects now while under their spell, have strange powers, stroke barren hens into laying, cure warts, staunch bloodflow, quell fevers; June drifting with her eyes closed as the old woman gazes at the girl's taut flesh beneath the spread of her warped, thin fingers with those two unblinking different-colored hooded eyes, the one ice-blue and the other coal-black. *I didn't open my eyes for three days and nights after getting borned*—as a child, June loved hearing Auntie recount this—*and when I finally did, everyone who'd come from miles around to see the infant who wouldn't open her eyes then saw me open them and saw too that spider that was sprawled across this one that's dark. And they let it be, they did, 'cause they knew better back when, there's reasons for things people have forgot about now-adays, so they let the spider be and after about a thousand babies run out of her, she just sank into my eye and gave me what they call in-sight, which always kept me from ever being caught up in anybody else's web. Which a lot of people spin, mind you.* Despite her closed eyes, June, still drifting, can feel Auntie's gaze upon her, the blue eye unfaded by age, the pupil of the dark eye indistinguishable, can see without opening her own eyes the crisscross of wrinkles etched into the old woman's cheeks, those deeper lines cutting from nostrils to mouth; and she breathes in Auntie's scent—of lanolin, of the barren yellow earth drying after the rains, of sweat and smoke—given off by her skin, her scalp, her hair, her clothes. Enveloped by this redolence, June drifts beneath those hands, feels the old woman's warm palms between the bones of her hips, feels her fingers lightly probing and pressing and mas-saging ever so gently and finally eliciting a response, summon-ing a flutter, then another, stronger.

Ah, Auntie says, breathes deeply, says again: Ah.

June looks into the old woman's hooded, inscrutable, two-colored eyes.

What is it, she whispers.

Well, *that,* Auntie says, is a baby. And seeing the girl's in-comprehension, she repeats herself. When June doesn't respond, she takes her hands from the girl's belly and leans back into her heels, asks: Do you know who done you?

Who—

I'm doing the asking.

Oh.

Times some women don't know. Some get drunk and don't remember, and some get ravaged by strangers, some's got more than one beau. I'm only asking because if you know who got you this way, you might start thinking on making your condition known to him.

June stares up at her, incomprehension giving way to confusion, panic. But he said nothing would happen, she says, promised nothing could.

Words don't always count for much. Depends on who's doing the speaking. Never mind the situation.

And Auntie said June would birth in late winter, early spring. That she wouldn't show for a while, that her mother wouldn't notice now or even a month down the line. Hell, Auntie pronounced, that woman—she never refers to June's mother by name—isn't attached to her own shadow most of the time, and anyways, there she goes. How Auntie could see through the faded newspaper taped onto her windows utterly perplexed June, always had; and so June got up and opened the door quietly and went out, stood in the wind and watched her mother sally down the drive and turn on to the road, walk off solitary, become smalled by the immensity of the landscape. If only she would return with Bo: Bo was June's only hope, for Ward was his friend, and he'd know where Ward could be found.

Which June didn't: she didn't even know Ward's last name. She'd waited for him to return on his own, although he'd never given any indication he would. He'd only ever come along with Bo that summer, sometimes in Bo's pickup, sometimes following Bo in a beat-up Buick that was dented and scraped and always in need of one repair or another, and he and Bo had made themselves welcome with her mother—they always brought liquor and food, they came on Friday nights and stayed weekends—and it was Bo her mother favored to the extent of stopping her walkabouts and so ended up with, June always making herself scarce until Ward tired of being odd man out and began paying attention to her, taking her—and himself—out of Bo and her mother's way.

Not that he always showed when Bo did. Not that he ever came by on his own. And he never returned at all after Bo split with June's mother, after what Bo claimed was the last straw the morning he woke up to find his pockets emptied and her mother and his wallet gone. June hadn't seen her leave, but she knew her mother wouldn't be back soon, that she'd be gone for as long as Bo's money lasted and maybe even longer, for she always returned with something in hand: cigarettes, liquor, some cash, often another man or men, most of whom seemed interchangeable. Unlike Bo, whom June had taken a shine to: he'd brought Ward into her life, after all, and he'd been decent with her mother, hadn't ever raised a hand to her never mind knocked her about, always showed up with groceries as well as a couple of bottles, and had twice brought June presents, once a kerchief, once a pair of oyster-shell barrettes. No, June told Bo, she didn't know what direction her mother might take; she'd never known, and as far as she could remember she'd always been told never to ask. You mean she's been walking out on you all your life? Bo queried incredulously as June helped him search through every drawer and cupboard for his wallet, knowing their efforts to be futile. Just about, June admitted. Well, he said, after they'd turned the trailer upside down for no reason, that's that. And she wanted to ask Bo then

Ward—he hadn't come around with Bo that weekend or the former—but she didn't, she'd never asked after him, for so far as Bo and her mother were concerned she had no reason to mention his name, as neither of them had any inkling of what had happened between her and Ward. Who had never made any promises, never said he loved her; but he'd said other things, and with his body, his hands, revealed to June what he didn't put into words, and that which she couldn't because she was incapable of dreaming such a language.

The day Bo called it quits with her mother, he gave June his telephone number and told her the name of the town he came from and said: Call me if she bothers to bring back my wallet, but sorry, she didn't even leave me any change, and it'll cost you long distance. And then she watched him drive away, take with him any hope on her part that Ward might return. When neither of them did, she was left with nothing but her longing, and that was bad enough until Auntie placed her ancient hands on June's belly and pronounced she'd gotten herself with child.

June considered, at the time, that this day was the worst of her life.

But she was wrong. Worse days came later, after the season grew cold and the skies grayed in an endless overcast behind which the sun's faint orb dragged from one horizon to the other, after the snows covered the barren landscape in a blanket of white, after her mother realized the condition her daughter was in and threatened to kill her, pelting Auntie's trailer—where June had taken refuge—with snowballs until the old woman stepped out and placed one palm atop the back of her other hand and pushed both in the direction of June's mother and warned: Throw one more, and I will curse you. June's mother swayed, rocked, glared, took a step back in a knee-deep drift—she had never known where the old woman was from either, or how she had ever come to be in this place, or whether, as was rumored, she was descended from medicine hawkers, circus folk, magicians, shamans—and finally leaned over her feet, let drop a mouthful of spit. Keep your damnations to yourself until the day I kill her, which won't be today and maybe not tomorrow, but there'll come a time, June's mother threatened. Begone, came Auntie's reply, and June's mother turned and stumbled toward the road in the ruts cleaved into the snow by that flatbed truck, and in the distance eventually disappeared into the promise of twilight. That was after the holidays that weren't, the new year drifting on beneath a fishbelly sky pinning down a coldness that grew denser with every passing day, June trapped by her heavying body and the frozen landscape trapped beneath winter's layers, the road narrowed by snowplow banks whose heights obscured the occasional passing of cars except at the drive's end, which Auntie and June had cleared; but at the sound of any engine during daylight, June was wont to step outside and wait for the moment it passed by the drive, always in the insane hope that Ward's ill-used and maybe even ill-gotten Buick would materialize. That he would come back to her, and for her. Which he didn't, and then she could no longer wait: she began to fear that this entrapment—her body, the season—would paralyze her, and knew she had no choice now but to make her own way, search him out. Auntie gave June an old satchel with a wooden handle that might have been in her family since the time of the carpetbaggers, saying she'd never had any use for it and wasn't considering moving anywhere anyway for the rest of her life, and she gave the girl what cash she could spare, enough to keep her fed for a few days and allow her to pay for a room for a night or two if she needed. They'd basted panels with buttons and buttonholes into June's jeans, which panels could be removed after she gave birth, and she had an oversize sweater and a man's pea-coat two sizes too large, boots, a woolen hat and mittens to wear; the satchel held what little else she had. She waited until the appearance of the two men with their flatbed truck, who—after spending the night—told her the direction in which she needed to go to get to Bo's town, then took her as far as they were going. She told Auntie she'd write, and for the first time asked the old woman's name, but Auntie replied that her people had never done such, that the few who'd ever bothered even learning their letters just scattered and were never heard from again. Not that that mattered, she said, because gone is gone.

Anyway, Auntie told her, you won't be coming back. If you don't find him, remember to head into the sun and keep going until the land gives out.

That was their goodbye, at the crack of a cold dawn on a day when her mother was again nowhere to be found, June with the satchel at her feet at the door's edge in the high old cab, the two men elbow to elbow and the truck cranking past the town, population now 647 minus one, where she'd sometimes gone to school; and beyond the town limits she saw that the land and sky were just the same as she'd ever known them to be, the endless overcast of the season above and the remnant moraine of a distant age's glacial movements lying still beneath the snows that belied their sculpting. Both stretched on and on, and the changelessness did not surprise, as it was all she'd ever known. They stopped once at a gas station and again where they left her at a junction, which they said saw more traffic than the road on which they'd come. They pointed her in the right direction, told her the names of places she'd pass through, and claimed that drivers would be hard-pressed not to stop for someone in her condition. But she walked the rest of that morning—during which not a vehicle passed her—having no idea how far she'd come or how far she had to go, with the wind blowing spindrift over the rippled, pitted world and eating into her back, and she'd reached no town at all when, finally, a pickup came from behind and began to slow as she turned to face it, and she got her first ride of several. At the end of each, she was dropped off at a convenience store or gas station, where she warmed herself within the aisles or office and waited for someone going in her direction to pull in, shyly asking them if they could drive her on, and so by day's end was close enough to where she was going that she walked the rest of the way, into the town's outskirts of junkyards and auto repair shops and empty lots that were fenced in and sometimes shouldered by clapboard homes and the occasional house trailer. Then, closer to the town's center, side streets and more homes, and on the main road—which became Cedar Street, for less than a mile—offices and clothing and hardware and grocery stores and secondhand shops and bars and diners. People were locking up their stores, walking the sidewalks, going into their favorite eateries or watering holes or heading elsewhere in trucks and station wagons and sedans whose make she couldn't determine, their headlights shining high beams in the dusk that deepened into night as she walked to what she considered to be the town's other outskirts, then wound her tired way back to the first diner she'd passed, the first bar, and—with that satchel in her hand and in that oversize peacoat and that woolen cap and mittens, with her frozen cheeks and glistening eyes and protruding stomach and now swelling ankles and feet within those clunky boots, looking much the mendicant wayfarer from another place and time—got up her courage to ask of anyone who looked at her straight from behind the counter or cash register or bar whether they knew the man she was looking for, whether they might know where she might find him.

When a bartender in a dive asked the drinkers mounted on stools if anyone knew Ward, she saw how the men took her in and then gazed at their glasses, some shaking their heads and others making no motion, no one saying a word; and she realized, feared then, that even if they knew everything about Ward they wouldn't say because they saw she was pregnant and knew the predicament he'd be in—perhaps the same some of them had once upon a time found themselves in and not for the better—if she managed to track him down. June, however defeated she found herself by this reaction, told herself it wouldn't be like that: those nights she'd spent with Ward were the only times in her life anyone had taken an interest in her, had wanted to be with her; he'd been funny and tender and had jokingly teased her, saying he'd desired her since the first time he laid eyes on her; she told herself—despite her gnawing fear to the contrary—that he'd be glad to see her now, that for one reason or another he just hadn't been able to come back to her; also told herself she had to believe this, even when at a diner a young pretty woman behind the register couldn't disguise her surprise when June said his name, then quickly looked off and studied the corner of the ceiling for a moment as though thinking hard before saying, Nope, never heard of him.

It was Bo she finally found. She'd kept his phone number all those months, and she dropped change into the public phone she finally came across and dialed the number, and the woman who answered said, Just a minute. There were voices in the background, and then a man said hello, and June suddenly realized she didn't know what to say, so that the man said hello again, this time as a question, which prompted her to ask,

Is this Bo? and he said, Yup. She told him who she was, and there was a long pause. I'm sorry, she found herself saying, my mother never brought back your wallet, I don't have it. Is that why you're calling? he asked, and she said, No, well, I need to find Ward. And Bo asked where she was and she told him, and he said to stay there, so she did, leaning against the inside of the booth and feeling the deadness of the cold seep into her bones, and after a while it seemed to her that she'd been waiting for hours and that she'd most likely be waiting for the rest of her life. She didn't see Bo park his pickup at the corner of a side street opposite where she stood in profile to him, didn't see him get out of the cab or walk toward her, just heard him say *Aw Jesus* at the sight of her.

He didn't need for June to say why she was looking for Ward. He made a phone call, telling the person on the other end of the line that he'd be there soon, then took June to his place, a one-bedroom over a grocery store, and the woman named Jeanie to whom he introduced her made a fuss over her and saw to it that she ate something and that she'd be comfortable sleeping on the couch. The next morning Bo left for work, and Jeanie made breakfast and told June to go ahead and use whatever she needed to shower, there was shampoo and conditioner, and then she too left and Bo returned around five and poured himself a shot of whiskey and gave her a grin. June said, Your girlfriend is nice, and he replied, Don't I know it, she's got me so hooked we're moving out next week and going back to where she's from. He didn't say where that was, just went and changed out of his work clothes and told her, C'mon, bring your bag or whatever you call it, and he drove her to a part of town she hadn't seen the night before, into a neighborhood that probably wasn't thought of as one — the run-down houses were far apart, the streetlamps few, hauling trailers and pickups and cars that had seen better days were snowed in in backyards—and stopped before a several-storied, ramshackle house of weathered slat boards and peeling window frames that had first and only ever been painted before she was born. She could see that additions had been built onto the place, jutting out like rectangular tentacles. Bo told her to wait in the pickup and he went in, and after a quarter-hour or so came back out and said, He'll meet us later, give him some time, then took her to a diner and told her the fare was on him. He watched her examine the prices on the menu, and when she ordered an egg sandwich he told the waitress to scratch that and bring them each some meatloaf with mashed potatoes and gravy, and they ate in silence until their plates were finished, when June ventured: So he's with someone else. Bo looked her in the eye and said, I can't rightly say, it's been a while since I washed my hands of him, just have some dessert. She looked down at her plate and shook her head, said, I've got no craving for sweets, it's the craziest thing, and when she looked up Ward was coming in through the door and walking over to them, with a movement of his head telling Bo to push over and sitting next to him across from her, not saying hello but running a hand through his hair and then resting back against the booth. So, he finally said, Bo tells me it's mine.

The remark crushed her. She'd never considered that he'd think or insinuate otherwise, and she felt herself reel as though from a blow; if she'd been standing she would have staggered; she hadn't known what she'd expected but it wasn't this. Even if it had come as a shock to him he should still have been the man she'd known, the one who'd been sweet to her, so attentive, the one who'd taken them both out of Bo and her mother's way; they'd spent nights together in that Buick watching for shooting stars and trailing the moon and driving to the loneliest places on the planet, listening to the radio and with him sometimes singing—he had a sweet voice—at other times telling her bits and pieces about himself, that he hadn't had much of a family life, his parents being divorced, and that he'd bummed around some after leaving home and that his only degree came from the school of hard knocks, that he'd done dishes in restaurant kitchens and roadwork on highway crews and had framed houses in places that didn't have buyers, that he'd done time in mines and factories and once in a county jail—for what he didn't say—and for a while broke mustangs, which he said were the orneriest animals on earth. You know, he'd tell her, I never talk to women like this, you're too young to understand but there'll come a time in your life when you're no longer a girl and you won't be wanting to listen to these things, you'll be wanting men to tell you other things, oh lord are you ever going to be trouble—let me stop now, tell me about your boyfriend. But June had none, had never had, and told him this without saying why, that her mother was trouble enough, that she'd seen men come and go all her life and that the best she could say about them was that the only thing they all had in common was a stubborn selfishness, none of them ever wanting anything more than to get drunk or high or both and bed her mother until the good times soured; and the worst she could say about them was that when those good times went south most of them had a penchant for violence, their rages sometimes turning the insides of the trailer upside down and at other times leaving her mother, who like a wildcat tried to give as good as she got, broken and bloodied. So June told him only that she'd never had a boyfriend and didn't say why, and after that he groaned and shook his head and told her she was every man's dream because she'd never even ever been kissed, good lord did she know what that meant, what that could mean to a guy, until finally she said: So kiss me. And June never forgot that kiss, remembered everything that happened after, remembered every moment of what occurred between them all through that summer and into the fall, when Bo called it quits with her mother. She sat facing Ward in the diner with a hurt, astonished look in her eyes and said with utter finality, It's ours.

She refused to cry, but she couldn't say anything more because of the lump in her throat. For chrissakes, Ward, Bo said, do the right thing. And Ward did, he took her back to his place in that rooming house and settled her into the private annex he rented, with its one room and a bathroom. The room had a single bed and a double electric burner plate atop a small table, above which hung a frying pan and one pot. There was a percolator, a clothes cupboard, one armchair, one naked overhead bulb; the bathroom had a tub and wash basin, towel hooks. The room was chilly until he turned on the electric heater. She sat on the edge of the bed and he told her he'd see her through the pregnancy and birth and maybe a few months thereafter but that that was all, and then he'd take her wherever she wanted to go, name it. From that first evening he held himself aloof, brokered no intimacy, set a pallet on the floor for himself that he rarely used because he rarely slept there, but he gave her a bit of spending money and saw to it that she fed herself. He told her never to enter the main house or any other annex, for the place was shared only by men, all of whom paid weekly rent and worked odd jobs or had seasonal employment or were just drifting through, except for the place's owner, who lived there too and wouldn't take kindly to the appearance of a pregnant female in their midst. When Ward came around, he checked in on her cursorily and then sat drinking and smoking and talking with the other men in the house—she could sometimes make out the voices of five or six others, carrying through the walls in the night—with whom she never came into contact except for the college dropout who aspired to be a national Frisbee-throwing champion and told her he'd once made a lot of money dealing specialized strains of fine Mexican and Vietnamese marijuana, the proceeds from which he was using to coast by. He'd seen her come and go from that annex room and one day simply waylaid her, said by way of introduction, Whoa, what in the world has Ward been hiding here, and he treated her with an almost awed reverence because of her impending motherhood, and—despite June's misgivings, for what would Ward say—took to taking walks with her into town.

Ward thought nothing of it, neither showed interest in nor softened toward her, never bridged the chasm between them with his body or words, never once rubbed the soreness out of the small of her back or put his hands on her belly to feel the baby kick, although at times she noticed him looking oddly at her, as if in morbid fascination, during that last month when she no longer fit into those paneled jeans and her belly had dropped so that she carried low. Because of those instances, she tried to convince herself that Ward might, in the end, become intrigued with the notion of fatherhood, just as she wanted to believe that after the birth they might make a go of it. She had nothing else to go on and was more than willing to take him as he was: detached, unbending in his refusal to reach for her, and mostly absent. And as she'd lived so much of her life in abandonment, she found desertion a normal state of being, and in her solitude she did what she needed to in order to prepare for the infant, bringing back from a secondhand shop an old but pristine baby carriage, buying a dozen cloth diapers and some safety pins, a half-dozen baby bottles, and hand-sewing and knitting clothes so small that she could hardly believe how tiny a newborn could be.

Her water broke on a day Ward wasn't present. She trespassed his command and got herself around the front of the house and knocked on its door, then entered without an answer and told an old man she'd never before seen that she was in labor and needed to go to the hospital. In turn, he shouted for the college dropout, who emerged from somewhere upstairs and took one look at her holding the bottom of her belly and somehow convinced the old man to lend him his car, which the old man did on the proviso that he drop her off and head back immediately. She gave birth almost as soon as she was moved from the emergency room into the maternity ward, and she — following Ward's instructions, but not to the letter; he'd wanted her to say she didn't know who the father was — said she knew who the father was but that he wouldn't claim the infant as his own, and so gave the baby her last name as well as its first. The college dropout brought a gift of a small stuffed bear to the hospital that night, he her only visitor. He said he'd have brought her butterflies in a jar if it had been the right season but of course it wasn't and also they weren't in Mexico, where he'd once seen monarchs, what a trip, there'd been billions of them covering the enormous trees that grew on mountainsides. His pupils were dilated, he couldn't sit still, and she listened to him in a twilight trance that was bruised darkly because Ward — the college dropout said he'd been told she went into labor — didn't appear.

He turned up for her and the baby's release from the hospital — given her age, not quite sixteen then but almost, someone had to sign for her as the hospital wouldn't allow her and the infant to leave on their own, especially as there was an account to settle—after making whatever monetary arrangement he could. He was hung over. He didn't say where he'd been. The staff insisted she and the baby be wheeled to the exit, but he didn't offer a hand when she stood or an arm to walk her to the car. He didn't help her into it and refused to hold the infant, saying that he wouldn't because he didn't want anything to do with it. His name is Luke, and he's our son, not an *it,* she told him, and the hurt in her voice gave him pause enough to slam the passenger-side door on her. They returned to the house in silence, and the college dropout came out through the front door as they got out of the car and headed toward the annex room in which she'd spent two almost solitary months and now would spend others on her own with an infant. Sonovabitch, Ward, the dropout shouted in greeting, what a lucky dog you are.

If Ward was, if he ever even entertained such a notion, he never let on, just did what he needed in terms of making sure she and the infant had a roof over their heads. She managed as fairly as she could—Auntie had told her what to expect, what to do, when to switch over to formula, how to test the warmth of heated milk, how to sterilize pacifiers and bottles and diapers, how to soothe rashes with cornstarch, how to tell a cry of hunger from a cry of colic, how to swaddle and soothe—and kept in mind that Auntie had said, Just do the opposite of what you imagine your mother did and give that baby something to hold on to.

Ward disappeared, remained absent for most of the time. He didn't say where he went, where he stayed. He came by whenever she reached the end of what money he gave her. He didn't make himself at home, never sat on the bed or in the armchair, and had, in that first week of Luke's life, rolled up and removed his pallet. He never looked into the baby carriage, never reached out to take Luke, but as the infant grew into a being—and how rapidly changes occurred—she occasionally caught a glimpse of melancholy in Ward's expression as he looked around at the lodgings he'd provided her, them. He kept his thoughts to himself and remained aloof, unlike the college dropout, who made a fuss over her and Luke and without whom she might not have managed to get through the late winter, that cold spring, the oddly cool, rainy, interminable and inclement summer, for he took it upon himself to shop and run errands for whatever she, they, needed. She finally mentioned this to Ward, saying: I'd rather you were here to help out. He met her eyes evenly before setting his mouth in a hard way and telling her: It shouldn't matter that I'm not. But it does, she replied, and he repeated: It shouldn't. I never promised you anything more than that I'd see you through, I'm doing as much as I'm gonna do and, like I've told you before, I'm just biding my time until you name where you want to go.

And when I do.

I'll get you there.

And then.

He looked off, looked back at her, shrugged. I can't say. But maybe—and here he did not lie, but June did not and would never imagine that he was considering walking away from that hospital debt he didn't want to pay anything more on than he already had—it'd be the best thing for both of us.

The next time he came by, June told him the Atlantic, said she'd never seen the ocean and had always wanted to, that that's where she wanted to go. No, not the Pacific, the Atlantic; yes, she knew it was a longer way off than the Pacific. She didn't say what she hoped, that if they went as far as possible, then maybe during the going and given the distance something in him would soften, that he'd be thinking throughout the drive or when they got to where they were going that there wasn't a reason in the world not to begin over; and as he'd said *Maybe it'd be the best thing for both of us,* she clung to those words to perish the fear that he'd strand her in a place they'd never seen, where they knew no one. And so she calmly told him her desired destination, and he said, Well, that's going to take some doing, I need some time to get shit together. She waited almost two weeks for him to do whatever it was he had to do while she chose among the paltry possessions she had and decided what the baby would need, and one evening he came back and told her he was throwing out the baby carriage, that it wouldn't fit with whatever else they were taking, and that they were leaving the next day. That evening she decided to leave behind that old, too-large peacoat, her worn-out boots and ragged mittens and cap, and carefully packed into a box two cups, a few utensils, peanut butter, a loaf of sandwich bread, crackers, powdered milk and baby formula, clean baby bottles and diapers, and late that night he came by and placed the box in the trunk along with a bucket of tools and her satchel holding the few clothes she possessed, a bag of the baby's clothes, and one suitcase of his own. Her heart sank upon seeing that suitcase, considering he couldn't have put much in it; but she told herself neither of them needed much, that people start over with less. He said he'd be back at dawn, and he was, standing a ways down the street, leaning on the Buick and staring off, keeping his distance from the rooming house as she made her way out the annex door with a thermos of coffee in the bag she had over her shoulder and the baby in her arms. She didn't know whether Ward had said his goodbyes to the owner, the other men. The college dropout had vanished—without a farewell—and June had no one but Luke to tell of their leaving.

The landscape remained the same for hours, an entire day, into that first night—which they drove through as they had that day, stopping only at rest areas and filling stations, stopping only when the baby grew cranky enough to warrant being walked, stopping only to eat and to buy sodas and to fill the thermos—and only after dawn began to subtly transform itself into something other than what it had been, what she had ever only known the land to look like, be, a crenellate flatness the color of dun, mostly barren of growth. That flatness, the colorlessness, gave out on the second day, with the soft rise and fall of prairies a hundred or more years earlier plowed over and now bearing expanses of wheat and corn as far as the eye could see, interrupted here and there by farms and hamlets whose houses had lawns and whose boundaries were rimmed by rows of poplars planted shoulder to shoulder to demarcate habitations from the endlessness of all else. State boundaries marked no change in the landscape from one side to the next of each invisible line, which confounded her into wondering how such boundaries had ever been determined in the first place, how irrational the decision seemed, to have ended and begun two states when the land flowed in the same manner through both; there were as yet no rivers as natural bounds, not through that second day and night. By the third afternoon, their stops more frequent now, she became afraid of Ward dozing at the wheel, of the engine overheating—she saw the gauge climb beyond the middle of the range, hover just above the red warning line—and so afraid of dropping Luke, for she had barely slept, that she trussed the infant against her skin, inside the shirt she wore. And was relieved when, late that afternoon, the landscape to her amazement becoming forested and the highway now flowing through the dip and rise of rolling hills, Ward said *Enough* and chose an exit and pulled off of the highway onto a secondary route, drove along until they came to a motel whose vacancy sign, an affair written on cardboard, was posted inside the office window. Ward told her to wait and went inside, then returned and drove them to a door marked with a painted number, and settled her and the baby in a dim room whose rug and bedspread and furniture were in various shades of brown and the walls tan and stained and the water in the sink and shower rusty. The room smelled of disuse. Ward took from the trunk what she needed and told her he'd be back, and he must have seen the desperation in her face because for the first time since she'd shown up in the town they'd left behind, he touched her shoulder. Then repeated: I'll be back.

He stayed true to his word, returning at dusk with a cold sixpack and a pizza. They kept the door open, despite the late-day chill, to air the place out, and after he'd showered she left in Ward's care the changed and fed baby lying on his back and reaching for his toes and gurgling in the middle of one of the two single beds. Ward popped open a beer and sat on the other bed and maybe even watched the infant as she showered and toweled down and got back into her clothes. There was no TV, no radio. He motioned for her to join him on the empty bed, and they ate pizza and she drank her first beer, shook her head at the offer of another. He finished off the pack and lay down, and before he went to sleep carelessly placed a hand on the small of her back. She sat stockstill, afraid to move away from or lean into his touch, until his breathing evened and his hand dropped. And then she lay beside him, telling herself this had to be a new beginning; for if it wasn't, it was nothing at all.

Which is what it was. During the next days there were no more overnights at motels, just rest area stops, with her and the baby now in the backseat and him in the front, sleeping where they pulled over for a few hours in the car and then driving on again, stopping for food and formula and water, Ward pushing the Buick no more than fifty to keep the radiator from overheating. The topography, the flora, the highway were beyond anything she'd ever dreamed, hills gave way to mountains, huge rivers were crossed and huge cities skirted, monstrous trucks tailgated and passed them, the traffic heavying and thinning, becoming dense again, lightening again. The baby in her arms exhausted her, and the going wore them down. On the sixth morning they stopped for breakfast at a diner and she took the baby into the women's room and in a mirror saw herself as pale, tired, and haggard as Ward, and when she rejoined him she asked if they shouldn't find a motel, sleep, but he didn't answer and they ate what they'd ordered and then he paid the bill and they continued on. The last part of that day was the worst. Ward's driving became erratic, she had to watch his eyes in the rearview mirror to make sure they didn't close, that he didn't lose focus, and they went almost as far east as they could before he turned north and left the interstate and began following signs to places she'd never heard of, small places, until he stopped and studied the map, then drove on and left the secondary route for an even smaller one, this less traveled than any road she'd seen since she'd walked out of her life almost a year before, and when that road swung them onto the coastline, Ward said: There's your goddamn ocean.

He didn't stop. She gazed at the water dumbly, unable to make sense of it, too tired to be overwhelmed, not even fully realizing that they'd reached an edge of the continent, unable to process the enormity of having come to the destination she'd chosen, because every cell in her body was crying out for sleep. To her relief, he finally pulled into Mabel's, and to her shock he asked to rent a cabin for ten days and pulled a thicker wad of bills out of his pocket than she had ever known anyone to have. And by the next morning, after the cloud of fatigue had lifted and she saw, sensed, more clearly, she reflected on that wad of bills and realized he had that much money on him for one of two reasons: either because they were actually going to make a go of it or because he alone had a need for it.

She didn't ask, and he didn't say. Days, nights, passed. He didn't touch her. He circumvented as best he could her nearness, barely tolerated her presence, paid no attention to either her or the baby except when standing in the doorway to keep a watchful eye out for Mabel, to whom he turned a cold shoulder and so barely acknowledged; but he kept up certain appearances, silently and morosely, driving them into the small resort community's strip mall and buying whatever June cautiously chose, leading the way on foot to the dunes and beach across the road from the cabins, occasionally telling her tersely that at one point she'd have to stop hanging about his neck if he was going to go look for a job. The first day he left her alone, she dreaded he wouldn't return, but he did. And then he drove off the next and—despite again telling her he'd be back—left for good.

She had forty-seven dollars and change to her name. And she waited through that first day, then the next, taking the baby to the ocean at daybreak. The third morning, she'd made her decision, and took the baby through the foggy chill that bit through her thin clothes, the infant wrapped up warmly and wide awake, chirping, gurgling, making eyes at her and laughing on their journey through the dunes, onto the beach, where she stood at the water's edge for a very long time before slipping off her shoes and stepping into the surf with Luke in her arms. The ocean as immense as the emptiness within her, its freeze cramped her feet, her calves, made her catch her breath and exclaim, hoist the baby—to whom she could give no father, no grandparents, no past or future; she'd lain awake all night, her mind churning with desperation because there was no one she could turn to and never would be—higher onto her shoulder. *Gone is gone. Gone is gone.* Thigh-deep, she braces against the swells, Luke now no longer laughing but squirming and crying as the waves soak through to his flesh, and he is so defenseless, so so small, that she dares not look at her son but concentrates on her determination and the roiling, terrifying pull of the undertow, the icy chill, her fear of the water's infinity and her relief at its promise, the ocean—like life—simply beyond comprehension because of its magnitude, its meaninglessness. She tells herself, teeth chattering and clinging to the struggling infant now wailing in her arms, better to do this, keep going, it'll take no time to freeze, to drown, and she stifles a cry, almost chest-deep and losing her footing she feels her body fight for its life, force her back, when she hears a rabid barking and so turns, sees a beast of a dog harrying the shoreline, racing to and fro in its shallows but looking directly at her, keeping her in its line of vision, the one sentient creature in the universe distressed by her immersion, Luke's screams, the only creature in the world to bear witness, away from which she takes another step backward into the deep as a swell lifts her, bobs her upward, sets her down and onto her feet in its trough. And perhaps her, their, disappearance at that instant maddens what might be an already insane creature; at any rate, the dog takes the plunge, dolphins in and out of the breaking surf until it can no longer touch the seafloor and then swims strongly toward them despite the waves breaking over its head, the dog relentless and, she suddenly realizes, watching in amazement as the ocean tosses her about, beautiful. Gorgeous, crazy, this scene, her view toward the shore, of that deserted beach whose edges and dunes disappear into fog, this lone dog with its massive seal-like head, ears flattened, trying to set right what is not, trying to rescue her or perhaps only the baby — she'll never know — and taking the chance it might follow them both to their deaths. And that realization, the magnificence of the creature's intent, moves her, Luke's cries move her, her own breathing takes on an unearthly sound not unlike the dog's, the beast so close now she can hear its keening, and as she grabs on to its tail the dog turns and strokes powerfully toward the shore.

And then they're in the shallows. She can't feel her feet or legs, lets go of the dog, stumbles onto the shore as the dog circles and whines, herds her farther from the ocean's edge until she falls to her knees and, gasping and shaken to her core, tries to hold on to Luke, for the infant is arching his back, arching away from her, pumping his arms, kicking his feet, his face wrinkled into a fixed wail and his lips blue, his skin translucent, his eyes rolling skyward. The dog pauses several times in its mad circling to shake itself off, then continues its herding, quieter now, no longer whining, as June tears at Luke's clothes and at her own and finally rubs the naked infant against her shirtless chest, envelops and rocks him, rocks herself as the sun begins to cut through the mist, its thin warmth kissing her back, the baby's crown, their skin, the dog's thick fur as the animal settles onto the sand and rolls over once, twice, then quietly watches mother and son. When it later gets to its feet, the dog noses her arm and licks her hands before trotting off up the coastline, continuing on its way but pausing frequently to toss a look back over its shoulder in their direction. As if to make sure that she, they, remain on solid ground.

She eventually lies down with Luke on her chest, in her arms. The dog does not return, disappears as any apparition, and although June never lays eyes on it again she will greet it with joy in those infrequent dreams in which the shaggy, huge creature appears over the course of the rest of her life, dreams she will never tell anyone, not even her son. When Luke's skin is dry, she sits up and pulls her wet shirt back on and swaddles the again-protesting baby, whispers and sings and carries him back to the cabin, where she bathes him, gently towels and dresses him, then strips and rubs herself down and changes her clothes, wrings out her hair, and eventually sits, remaining stunned for much of the quiet day that passes before she enters the office and tells Mabel that she and Luke have been left behind, that Ward is not coming back.

When Mabel replies, *It's just as well,* June begins to weep—that decade of tears she holds within her is no longer dammed, there is nothing she can do to stop the flow—not only because of the woman's hard, if kind, response, but because of that monstrous, almost magical dog that has saved two lives for no reason she can possibly fathom.

Iris

MABEL WAITS FOR IRIS, who from upstairs had called out to her that she'd be down in a bit, that she'd lost track of time, although Mabel wonders how that could be the case as Iris had obviously risen to unlock the outside door to what Claire had always termed, without ruefulness or resentment, Iris's compound. Not an unfitting description in one respect, Mabel thinks, for the high concrete wall—smooth as pewter, and gunmetal gray—that extends from the house to enclose the entire property gives the impression of impregnability from both inside and out. June had blanched slightly at the sight of it and of Iris's house, which from the street appears to be a windowless bunker adjoined to that wall. There's hardly any frontage, just a short flagstone drive announced by a mailbox whose sole identification reads 154, and the drive ends at the wall—Iris had had the carport that was once attached to the house dismantled—in front of the only entrance door, which, despite being made of wood and its remarkable size, happens to be painted the same shade of gray as the concrete and so might be mistaken for a tromp l'oeil by discerning passersby or missed altogether by the undiscerning. What frontage isn't flagstone-paved lies sterile beneath a spread of bluestone chips.

And Mabel hadn't said anything to assure or warn June that there was no describing the paradox she was about to encounter within, but smiled when June caught her breath after entering through the gray door. Waiting for Iris now, Mabel marvels at that paradox, Iris's paradise, Mabel sitting within Iris's livingroom and looking out through the French doors at the patio crested by a wisteria-covered pergola, and beyond that at the almost two acres of garden contained within that wall—hardly seen for the ivy and bushes and trellises of roses and morning glories and flowering creepers Mabel has no names for—that hems out the forest beyond and, as intended, deprives anyone of the possibility of prying. Within the garden, at its far end, a long wooden leanto backed against the wall harbors cordwood culled from every tree—maple, oak, cedar, ash—that had once graced the lawn, of which not one blade of grass remains; and while the cordwood fills three quarters of the leanto, the other quarter comprises an enclosed shed that holds rakes and shovels and gardening tools, bushel baskets, stools, hoses, watering cans, pans and canning jars. Closer to the house but not facing it, looking onto the garden from its own angle, is what had been the original house on the property, a one-room cottage with a severely pitched roof so high that a person in its sleeping loft can stand tall; and the cottage too has a porch, its shingled overhang supported by four cypress trunks whose bark was lopped off and their circumferences made uniform with an adze. Until Matthew died, the cottage, that original structure, hadn't been lived in for decades and instead housed the castoffs of a previous time, harnesses and grain storage bins and horse blankets and milking pails, a wooden trough, all of which Iris had had carted away before she gutted and made the place livable—installing cabinets and closets and counters and electric heat and a kitchen alcove and bathroom and shower, restoring the fireplace and chimney, replacing windows and adding shutters, then furnishing the place spartanly—for herself, to inhabit alone during the months it took for the main house to be gutted, redesigned, rebuilt and refurbished. She made the cottage into a perfect guesthouse, and—as Iris would never have admitted to being prescient, to so much as thinking about Claire in those months never mind assuming that Claire would choose to live there—for the necessary duration felt herself a guest, a stranger, amid the detritus of a world she was intent upon, and succeeded in, destroying.

And re-creating: this, the wonder of it all, Mabel thinks, looking out over the garden's trees—apple and apricot, pear and persimmon and cherry, dogwood and rhododendron, weeping birches, Chinese maples, sumacs, blue firs and creeping junipers—interspersed among beds of yarrow, black-eyed Susans, echinaceas, asters, tiger lilies, peonies, roses, sunflowers, zinnias and chrysanthemums. Cobblestone paths whose edges sprout with spider grasses and herbs lace the grounds. Within and without, nothing of the house or acreage, but for foundations and bedrock, is as it was before Matthew died.

Iris has not stepped out beyond these walls except to gather the mail since the year after his death. She sits upstairs, fighting back the nausea that has plagued her since waking, for close to dawn, once again, she dreamed her recurring nightmare of burying Matthew, again. It is always the same: his open grave, on a knoll, yaws pitch-black beneath a sagging cobbled sky that cannot be trusted not to give way, plummet piecemeal onto the heads of the living, obliterate all trace of them. The burial service is taking place in the midst of disorder; the surrounding tombstones, haphazard, tilted, or toppled and prone, are somehow portentous of worse to come. A flyblown mutt, dog of hell oozing maggots on the pile of earth pyramiding the foot of Matthew's grave, raises its head to stare sightlessly through leaf-strewn eyes at what it cannot see. The knot of cowled, dark-garbed mourners, slope-shouldered as vultures, fix the dog with a beady gaze until as a flock they become restless, apprehensive, cock their hooded heads and cast their eyes at the heavens whose netlike stitching holding the sky intact begins to unravel. One by one, two by two, by the dozen—in the way of dreams there is no accounting, no possible logic—the flowingly caped funeral-goers flap their arms, take their hurried leave as the deadeyed dog pushes onto its bony sore-infested haunches, lifts its nose, opens its muzzle in mute howl. Flies erupt from its fanged jaws, the fiend is voiceless, the flies as insidiously silent. As if signaled by the pests, a cassocked priest opens his missal. This, an ominous cue—here Iris always becomes agitated, struggles to wake from the nightmare, but the dream's sequence is immutable, dreadful, repetitive, she knows the netting is about to split but fails to break through sleep's veneer, although the mesh tears with a deafening resonance and the dream's only sound becomes the thunderous timbre of canvas shredding. At this, the priest snaps the missal shut without having glanced at a passage and palms it in one hand, extends the other to point at Iris and then at the hole in the ground, Iris helpless as a puppet, her eyes directed by the gossamer pull of the priest's gesture. She never wants to look, and terror fills her because her eyes are commanded to do so, and what she sees is always the same: there is no coffin, Matthew's putrefied flesh is curiously waxy and almost indistinguishable from the leaden chains binding his arms to his torso, the padlocks huge, a leather cord biting into the swollen flesh of his neck; there is no coffin, and Matthew is blue-gray and swollen and horrific, trussed and throttled and naked but for the hood over his head and but for the flies attending his flesh.

He is the way he was when Iris in life found him dead.

She always needs to scream through the dream to wake herself, but can never manage; she always feels herself open her mouth wide, wider—always senses this, for the nightmare at times is more delirium than dream—as the first cobblestone falls from above, a second, before the sky caves and avalanches. Whatever the ether appeared to be it no longer is, and the cobblestones tumbling to earth are strangely unsolid, they hit with great thuds, splat with the consistency of wet clay and split with ooze, knocking the hellhound from its feet and burying it alive, secreting the tumbled tombstones in sludge, besmirching the priest's vestments, sullying Iris's dress. The priest scoops a handful of wet earth, wet sky, from within Matthew's rapidly filling grave and stands over Iris. She never knows how she comes to be on her knees in the nightmare, there are moments of pure disembodiment, but she is still openmouthed. Instead of screaming, she extends her tongue as if to receive communion. The priest incants nothing, and he is never gentle. The mire tastes of fluvial rot and decayed flesh and makes her stomach heave, but Iris cannot retch because the priest has filled her mouth with putrefaction and holds a monstrous hand over her face as she is smothered, asphyxiated, burned by the bile rising in her throat.

The bile is always real. Was upon waking.

Iris finally rises from where she sits on the edge of her bed, steels herself to go downstairs, face Mabel. She can still taste the bitter residue of the bile, swallows hard, examines herself in the mirror. Khaki work pants, khaki work shirt: her wardrobe consists of nothing but, has consisted of the same like sets of pants and shirts — some in gray — since she moved back into this house. A face too thin. One arm with a slight tremor, today not quite noticeable. Her left leg doesn't drag behind her, though she has the impression it does and so comes down the stairs placing her left foot first. She motions for Mabel to stay where she is, says: I'll make tea. She thinks to confess the reason for her delay, describe what it's like to struggle to swallow liquefied brimstone, suppress the fiery slurry of reflux, thinks to tell Mabel that this nightmare which came from nowhere some weeks ago now recurs with unnerving frequency. To admit she now despairs of losing that peace she created for herself by withdrawing from the world after burying Matthew, of instead remaining in this world within his grasp. To rail how unfair, *how unfair,* after all these years and after all she'd done to wipe the slate clean, to now be cursed with this dream of burying him again. After all, she'd seen to it that the coroner ruled Matthew's death accidental, no easy task, so that the priest could say a funeral Mass and then accompany the casket and mourners to the cemetery and bless the gravesite, sprinkle holy water one last time, read one last psalm; the cemetery had been perfectly manicured, there had been no flyblown netherworld dog, no overturned tombstones, no strangers dressed like carrion birds; the sky had not collapsed, no one had rammed muck from Matthew's open grave down Iris's throat, and Matthew's coffin had remained closed. Though, truth be told, for all Iris knew he might have been naked within, bound in that wrap of padlocked chains and that cord wound about his neck, that hood over his head, the way she'd found him.

She had refused a wake with an open casket. Why look at the dead. Why. To know what is not sleep, to know what is already known.

Matthew's eyes had to be sewn shut.

Matthew's death, of which she'd emptied herself for years, remained fable beyond Iris's insularity. Because people have a penchant for sensationalism, the tale became even more ghastly in its telling over time—so little out of the ordinary happened in the town then, Matthew's demise occurred before the era of random drive-by shootings and not-so-random murders, and long before townsfolk thought to lock their doors even when they were at home or began to lay wages on how long any cashier working the lobster shift at the local 24/7 store might survive before some lone customer in the deep of night did violence to her—and a milestone in the town's mythology. And Iris knew she'd never be able to extricate herself from that. She never considered that the aspersions—actual or imagined—cast on her were anything but inescapable: she'd felt herself tainted for life, had from the moment of Matthew's burial, when all niceties had finally been exhausted. She also never considered, no matter the passage of the past, that she might ever be anyone but the woman whose husband had been found. In such a way as.

He'd left her no choice: Iris determined that before Matthew's wake. And stayed true to that determination after his funeral, to never again face anyone who knew him or heard tell of his death, and the latter included a good number of townsfolk who, despite best intentions, tend like all people to be unwittingly pitiless because they are for the most part bored, and to be essentially cagey because for the most part callous; and Iris was terrorized by the thought, no, her knowledge, that stories would circulate and that whispers would follow in her wake if she were so much as glimpsed anywhere. She was convinced that her presence in public would forever arouse furtive and outrageous conjecture behind her back, and that no coroner's ruling, no priestly complicity, and no amount of time would soften the truth—not that the truth could ever be known—or settle wagging tongues. For Matthew had managed to die in a lurid, indecent, wholly obscene and inconceivable way, in the throes of some unconscionable act he was performing nude, chained, hooded, and—ostensibly, according to the police—alone. That being known as fact by the authorities, the priest, and the undertaker, Iris feared, correctly, that word would get out, that speculation would never be stemmed, and so resolved to avoid rather than inspire those rumors that the collective imagination would let run rampant. She once told Mabel she'd had no choice because she was incapable of removing herself, removing Matthew, from the gossip mill: she could only minimize her exposure by refusing to ever again acknowledge or be acknowledged by anyone in the town where she'd been born and brought up. Which was why, during the wake and funeral, Iris nodded speechlessly at people's condolences, rebuffed with silence their attempts at commiseration, shrank from everyone's touch, and hid her impenetrable grief behind impenetrably dark glasses, seeing through them darkly, indistinctly, knowing she had already steeled herself for what had just become the rest of her life.

Everyone assumed that Iris's behavior belied her shock. But she was not in shock: she was infuriated and unforgiving. For Matthew's death set before her the task of banishing all memory of him in order to quash her outrage at having lived with

someone she came to consider a monster and her rage at having
been widowed in this way. She left Claire—to whom Iris would
remain as good as dead—with Mabel and Paul for the better
part of a year. In the first week of her widowhood she changed
her telephone number and had it unlisted; shredded and burned
her wedding photographs and every other photograph in which
Matthew appeared; tossed Matthew's clothes and toiletries into
boxes along with what clothes he had ever given her or had
ever seen her wear and brought those boxes to the town dump;
donated what furniture, rugs, curtains, linens, towels, knickknacks, plates and glassware, cookware and silverware they'd
accumulated together to a Goodwill shop. Iris's activities did not
go unnoticed, and Claire did not go unmissed, and so the town
was rife with rumors that Iris intended to move. But a move
was out of the question, for Iris could not bear the thought of
starting over: new neighbors would be intrusive even if kindly
in their welcoming; there would be questions as to where they
were from, who they were, how they liked their new surround-
ings; and Iris would have to uproot Claire, she'd be expected
to enroll her daughter in a new school, attend parent-teacher
meetings, live a normal life—which she could not imagine leading—perhaps even be considered, after the requisite period of
mourning, as an eligible widow. Instead, Iris traded in what had
been their car, a sedan, for a station wagon at a dealership in another town, and in the same town sold her wedding band and
engagement ring and every piece of jewelry Matthew had ever
given her, then went to a hairdresser who'd never seen Iris before and certainly never saw her again, to cut her brown shoul-
der-length hair short and frost it. She gave out her unlisted telephone number to Mabel, and to Duncan, whom she'd sought out
to handle the estate; Matthew's several insurance policies—he'd

been an insurance salesman, after all—came to an extraordinary amount of money Iris never expected (she hadn't even known about the policies until after Matthew had been buried) and barely dented with the renovation of the cottage and house, the clearing and replanting of the garden, the final construction of that wall, higher than the height of a tall man standing on the shoulders of another, which could have served in another time and place as a stockade.

Iris turned her back on their friends, their acquaintances, the town, and Claire, who finally returned from Mabel and Paul's, only to find the house she had once known now entirely reconstructed and unfamiliar, emptied of everything she'd grown up with. Iris took no pity on her, indeed could hardly bring herself to look at Claire, because she needed to shield herself from that last vestige of Matthew. For Claire resembled him, and Iris needed no reminders: it was enough that when alone she was still being stunned at the oddest moments by the sudden recall of his face, the scent of his skin, the shape of his ears, his hands, the sound of his voice, the way he breathed and laughed, walked, held a martini, publicly charmed their friends, and privately humiliated her. It took more than a decade—Claire by then long gone and Iris long perfectly insular—to quell those unwelcome and unbidden shock waves that sometimes surged through and froze her with the same paralytic fright she'd experienced at having found Matthew beside that overturned stool, his garroted and strangely waxen body bloomed with splotches the color of amethyst, him vilely lewd, slightly bloated, stiffly contorted—perhaps there'd been a struggle of sorts; at any rate, he was twisted, one heel resting on a leg of the overturned stool as if he had attempted to reach it, gain some purchase, or perhaps his body simply fought its own demise—in the throes of rigor mortis.

Death by magic.

Have you told Claire? Mabel asks, coming up behind Iris, who stands with a hand to her mouth in front of the steeping tea. Iris turns to her with a look of surprise, as though she hadn't realized Mabel was even present, for she is in the grip of those images from the inexplicably recurring nightmare and of her memories of Matthew's death, which she had so long ago successfully repressed. Told Claire what? Iris asks.

About the girl staying here over the winter.

Oh. Well, it's such a minor matter, there's no reason. Besides, she wouldn't be interested in the least.

And with that she brings the teapot to the table, Mabel following with cups and saucers she takes from the open shelves that line part of the kitchen wall. Iris uses both hands to pour, settles back in her chair, leaves her cup untouched.

How long has it been now?

Since we spoke?

No. The tremor.

I haven't kept track. Some days I hardly notice it.

And you won't see a doctor.

I'd rather operate on the principle that what I don't know won't hurt me. Besides, the only doctor I'd trust to come over probably isn't making house calls anymore, if he's even alive.

Well, at least June can be of some help. If you need it.

What I need, Iris says, is to manage on my own.

And, Mabel reflects, that is all Iris has ever needed since Matthew's death, and accomplished to perfection, removing herself from life at the age of thirty-seven. No, a year later, Mabel corrects herself, for in that first year of Iris's widowhood she still drove, albeit to other towns for what she needed, and she'd no choice but to tolerate the workmen and landscapers she'd hired from elsewhere to renovate the house and cottage and re-move the lawn, plant trees, deliver and lay cobblestone and flag-stone and bluestone chips, erect that wall. By the time Claire re-turned, that station wagon was gone, sold or given away, for Iris had no intention of ever leaving the premises again, and had never a need to. For Duncan—who undoubtedly was able to financially survive his first few years as the new lawyer in town because of Iris's retainer—arranged everything, as Iris had charged him to, from bill-paying to grocery deliveries and garbage removal (for trash, back then, still had to be taken to the town dump) to Claire's schooling and doctor and dentist ap-pointments. Iris, so far as Mabel knew, refused to have even a checkbook on hand, and it astounds Mabel to think that nearly two decades have passed since Iris got rid of the station wagon, fourteen years since Claire left, and that in those intervening years only Duncan and Mabel—both, rarely—have had the privilege of passing through that outside door. Until now.

She won't bother you, Iris.

That's what Duncan said.

I could ask her to join us.

Oh, Iris tells her, finally reaching for her tea, I'd rather wait.

Mabel had known that this wouldn't be easy, that Iris would be even more uncomfortable at being left with June than the girl could possibly imagine, that Iris has no idea what to say to her, how to be with her, for she doesn't want to be confronted by anyone with whom she'll be obliged to speak and whom she won't help but see; and Mabel knows too that Iris finds it im-possible that the girl won't be a bother, for the only way June wouldn't bother would be if she were invisible. Like, in her own way, Iris has been, except with Mabel—who seldom visits—and Duncan, with whom she speaks almost exclusively over the telephone, Duncan always initiating a monthly call to give Iris an accounting despite knowing that she is not interested in figures or in answering his question as to how she is, which since she'd retained him has never varied from a curt *Fine, thank you.* So Mabel helps herself to more tea and settles into telling Iris how the season went, watches Iris begin to relax, to warm to her company, for they're comfortable with each other as only long-time friends can be, neither of them bothered by the silences that fall between Mabel's description of June and July and August, of the way rentals this year fell off: there's the inconvenience of her location—the beaches without lifeguards, the fact that you have to bring your own groceries and drive elsewhere to replenish them, drive off for entertainment and not that there's much of that in the small beach town a ways down the road, plus there's the gas crisis and the faltering economy. Times have changed, Mabel tells Iris, the families who used to come no longer do, a lot of the old regulars now have camps on the lakes up north, and the highway has taken its toll; only the locals and the lost now use the old post road that runs past Mabel's place. Or so it seems to her.

But you'll open again in the spring.

I wouldn't know what else to do. Plus I've promised June—not just you, Mabel adds—that I'll take her back then.

And there's Roland, of course, Iris remarks.

Roland, Mabel muses aloud, will do what he always does and just ignore that closed for the season sign. And Iris wonders if Mabel has ever suspected that Roland is waiting out her mourning—there's no other explanation for his constancy—although he must surmise, and be oddly at ease with the suspicion, that Mabel might never stop grieving. But mourning is not something Iris can discuss, not with anyone and certainly not with Mabel, for if Iris regretted Matthew's death she did so not with sorrow but with a relentless vehemence that bordered on hatred because of the way he died and—although Iris has never said and would probably never tell anyone—because of who he became, was, before he died. No, Iris never once considered Matthew's death tragic—which Paul's was—and its insidiousness sealed her fate. She accomplished what she saw as her only possibility and withdrew from the world, and has made her peace with that. Unlike Mabel, she wants no reminders of her past, has refused all intrusions, and reflects now that, despite their friendship and what they've long had in common, she and Mabel could not have suffered widowhood more differently, which has made them unique to each other.

My guess is, one day that man will ask you to marry him, Iris says, corrects herself: No, Roland won't ask. He'll just say *Marry me*.

Mabel shakes her head, almost laughs in disbelief. Well, before that happens, I'll have to introduce you to June.

Oh.

It's time, Iris. She won't come over on her own, believe me.

And so they rise, Iris sensing the drag in her leg and ignoring what she tells herself cannot be seen, this annoying lag, and follows Mabel as they cross the garden along the one cobblestone path Iris so painstakingly placed on her own. She stands back from the cottage porch while Mabel knocks at its door, which the girl opens quickly and slips out from, tall and impossibly angular and shockingly young, appearing far too young to have had a child, with that face forcibly composed in an expression of calmness because she is anything but. June's eyes are red and swollen, Mabel realizes she's probably been crying since stepping inside: there wasn't much else for her to do, for Duncan made sure that the cottage was perfectly set up—the place was spotless, he'd put in a crib and highchair, stocked the shelves; there are pots and pans and dishware, a portable television with rabbit ears, a radio, blankets and sheets, towels, dishrags, soap and dishwashing liquid and laundry detergent, fresh bedding at the foot of the daybed as well as the loft bed, and twenty-five dollars with a note from Duncan describing how things worked and instructing June to come to his office at three o'clock on Friday. June and the baby had few enough possessions; it wouldn't have taken more than minutes to put their belongings in drawers and the closet, make the beds. Mabel introduces June, still standing in front of the door, to Iris, still standing beyond the porch, and they manage an awkward hello, freeze into silence.

And Luke? Mabel queries.

Sleeping.

He's a good baby, Mabel says to Iris.

Well, that's fine, Iris responds.

And Mabel thinks: *This is awful*. Says, to dispel her own dread: Let's show June the garden.

Iris leads the way. June brings up the rear. They walk wordlessly over the paths that wind through the trees and flowers, bushes and grasses, which Mabel assumes correctly June has no names for, wondering all the while whether Iris has realized, is realizing, how different this tentative, childlike girl is from Claire, who was never tentative and never quite childlike even when small because of the way she had of viewing and absorbing the universe, as though she were born with foreknowledge or could identify because of unambiguous recall from a previous life those things she effortlessly familiarized herself with once again. Claire at six—or perhaps seven, at any rate very young, and intensely curious despite having a relaxed manner born of natural wisdom—speaking as lucidly as an adult, besting Paul at checkers, Paul not giving an inch and the child still winning, explaining as well that the rules by which he played didn't exactly follow what was written on the inside of the box, but that that was okay by her; and knowing the names of birds and trees and shells by then, able to roll a quarter between her fingers and make it disappear before pulling it out from behind Paul's ear, and by the time she turned eight teaching herself chess, teaching Paul too, and already a mean blackjack and cribbage player. She confounded Mabel and Paul during the year she stayed with them, at twelve able to identify the constellations and to trace on any map the plates responsible for continental drift and to recite the classification of species, geological eras, the topographic layers of the earth's crust. Before Iris even planted the fruit trees and flowers and grasses and shrubs, Claire could probably have named them all: that was the way she was, born seemingly without a clean slate, and here June—who, it occurs to Mabel, probably hasn't even ever seen an actual apple, pear, persimmon, or apricot tree—had nothing but. Unless becoming pregnant and carrying full-term and birthing and knowing in some rudimentary way how to look after an infant could be discounted. Which, Mabel figures, maybe could be: even with the knowledge of such, the girl is otherwise so unsure of herself and wary of her own uncertainty, of her own ignorance, that she's kept everything she knows—if anything—and everything she's been through, to herself. They wind through the garden slowly, Mabel doing the talking that Iris—who hasn't had anything to say to anyone, Mabel and Duncan and Claire excluded, for almost twenty years—cannot or will not, and hearing her words fail to provoke any acknowledgment from a girl who must feel, not for the first time, unwanted and consigned to silence. Mabel pauses by the leanto and explains that the shed holds gardening tools, then asks Iris whether June should take on the task of stacking cordwood onto Iris's patio.

Well, Iris says, without looking at either of them, I don't see why she should.

Maybe there's something else—

Not a thing, Iris snaps. The tone of her voice—she hasn't looked at June—freezes the girl, but Mabel recovers immediately, smoothes over that snarl, gently says: I'd trust June to her own judgment, Iris. You two can work things out later. It's about time for lunch—I've brought sandwiches—so, June, go on and get Luke and bring him over to the house. And June looks at Mabel beseechingly, at Iris's turned back, and Mabel nods at her, touches her shoulder, sends her off, waits for Iris to stop studying the cordwood as though her life depended on inventorying the stack. I'm not going to be good at this, Iris finally says.

We'll have lunch, Mabel says, and then I'll bring her into town, let her get her bearings, and by the time we get back it'll be late afternoon, and she won't bother you, not then and not tomorrow and not the day or week or month after that.

See to it.

I will.

And during lunch Mabel can tell from Iris's posture and face, that tremor in her arm, the way gravity rounds her shoulders and curves her spine, that Iris is defeated, drained. June sits straightbacked, almost on the edge of her seat, holding the baby on her lap with one arm and nibbling primly at a sandwich, and the baby — now awake — watches Iris so intently that she can't help but notice, although she doesn't make a move or sound that could possibly signify that she's returning his interest. Luke — as if amused — grows more and more animated, gurgling and laughing and staring at Iris, flinging his hands in the air, kicking his feet. I'll clear the table, June finally says, and Mabel tells her, Here, give him to me, June without hesitation handing Luke over as though Mabel — who has never before offered — is used to holding the baby. And as June clears the plates and returns for the glasses and silverware, Luke reaches constantly toward Iris and makes funny noises of sheer infant joy, until Iris finally softens, cocks her head to one side, whispers an exasperated *What?* in Luke's direction, which sets the baby to laughing and bouncing, Iris now shaking her head and repeating *What? What?* And Mabel is reminded, for the first time in many years, of how beautiful Iris once was, how lovely her features. Here, Mabel says, offering Luke up, and to her surprise Iris reaches out and takes him, despite that trembling arm, and raises him to her eye level, gives him a shake, wobbles him up and down in the air. The sight of which stops June in her tracks.

Luke's made a friend, Mabel says.

Don't count on that, Iris tells the infant. When she turns him around and places him on her lap, he glimpses June and screams in delight, raises his arms to her. He'll tire you out, June says.

Well, take him then. And after June picks the baby up, Iris reaches into a pocket and produces a key on a ring, holds it toward the girl. You'll be needing this, she says. Make sure to always lock the outside door whether you're going or coming.

Yes, ma'am, and thank you.

Don't thank me, Iris tells her, and don't call me ma'am.

Later, Mabel lets the car idle as she waits for June to disappear into what even Mabel now thinks of as Iris's compound, to close and lock the door behind her, and when the girl is gone Mabel shifts into reverse, backs out into the street, pulls away. She isn't sure whether she should feel relieved or rattled at having made this arrangement, but what's done is done. June was quiet as Mabel drove her around the area, to town and through it, Mabel slowing to point out where June would catch the bus and where she would get off nearest to Duncan's office, which she also pointed out, and then showing her the stores and diners and the one restaurant on the town's main street as well as the stores on the side streets, asking whether there was anything she needed to shop for now. There wasn't. The baby fell asleep before they reached town, remained sleeping the entire way, so that Mabel spoke in a low voice and told herself June was mostly silent because of Luke. But when they pulled back into Iris's drive, June hesitated, and Mabel almost held her breath thinking the girl would never make a motion to leave the car. Finally June said: I don't know what to call her or what to say to her.

Call her Iris, Mabel told her, and just go on with your life and take care of Luke. Iris hasn't had anyone around for years, so it'll take some time for her to get used to the idea.

Should I stack some wood tomorrow?

You might think about it.

June nodded, finally reached for the handle and opened the door. Mabel put her hand on June's arm and stopped her. She didn't know how painful it might be for the girl to hear the one question Mabel hadn't been able to bring herself to ask and now needed to. June, she said, what do you want me to do if he shows up and wants to know where you are.

The girl turned and looked at her in surprise. Goodness,

she said, he drove me and Luke clear across the country knowing my only hope was that we might make a go of it if we got
far enough away from where we'd started, with Ward—Mabel hearing for the first time June speak his name, which was
not the name on the license he'd handed to Mabel—not saying
we could or couldn't, just asking where I wanted to go, and we
got as far as we got and then he left us stranded without saying
a word, and left us with nothing. He just drove right off, and he
isn't coming back.

But if he does.

June pulled Luke to her, kissed the crown of his head,
the sadness coming over her face and into her eyes before she
averted them, sighed. Mabel, she said, just tell him we drowned.

Oldman

DUNCAN HADN'T FORGOTTEN June's first Friday appointment but he wasn't paying attention to the time because Oldman had come by with two hero sandwiches and a couple of cold beers to treat Duncan to a late lunch and tell him how he'd gotten a call from Dan Evans a few days back, and anything to do with Evans would, Oldman knew, be of interest to Duncan because Duncan had, without asking a penny, taken on Evans's case after Evans came walking—in a manner of speaking—out of the center for physical rehab, which no one but Evans ever expected he would. The accident he'd been in had flipped his pickup truck when the hitch to the camper he was hauling—which camper he'd hauled before and which hitch was certified to pull a lot more weight than what the camper weighed—had split a moment or two after Evans had pulled out of a filling station and was adjusting his seat belt the way people do, tugging at it before fastening

it. The camper and pickup jackknifed, the trailer toppling and
coming apart as it crashed, the pickup continuing on, skidding
along on its cab roof, with Evans not buckled in and his scalp
opening against the cab's ripped ceiling while his neck took
the brunt of the blows. His wife, Sharon, had fastened her seat
belt and ended up upside down without a scratch, but by the
time she managed to free herself from the belt someone who'd
been behind them by about a quarter-mile was already at Evans's door trying to pry it open. Evans was screaming at him to
shut the engine off, but the guy was so shocked at the amount
of blood coursing from Evans's scalp and at being yelled at that
he just kept pulling at the door, whose window had been broken out, as Sharon was still trying to unhook herself. The guy
finally screamed back at Evans, Buddy I'm just trying to get
you out—I don't know how to cut the engine but this vehicle
is going to blow, when Evans changed tactics and calmly told
him: Look, Bozo, just reach in and turn the goddamn ignition
key off. Which the guy did, then at Evans's bidding drove to
the first highway emergency phone and called in the accident
and said the driver was in a bad way, that his wife was trying
to stem the blood that was coming out of his head and that the
driver claimed he couldn't feel or move his legs and that he
didn't want anyone but medics touching him, never mind pulling him out of the truck. Evans later told Oldman and Duncan
both that he knew he might not live, but the thought of dying at
that moment just didn't sit right because he'd be leaving Sharon
in a mess, what with all the equipment he had in their yard—a
small backhoe, a tractor, the snowplow, a couple of snowmo-
biles, a shed and garage full of a lifetime's acquisition of carpen-
try tools—not to mention the debt they seemed never to quite

climb out of, which is why he'd sold the camper in the first place and was hauling it to the person who'd paid him extra to deliver it. Sharon rode in the ambulance with him after the medics had braced his neck and back and wrapped his skull, but the nearest emergency room couldn't handle Evans's grievous injuries, and she didn't get helivacked with him to the hospital that was part of a teaching college in the north of the state, where he was operated on and stabilized and, eventually, told by his surgeons that they hadn't quite expected him to survive and really couldn't explain why some feeling was coming back into his feet and legs. They shipped him out to a rehabilitation center as soon as they were sure his neck, which had been fractured in four places, had healed enough. At the center, Evans fumed at his arms and legs that had so quickly lost muscle, at the skin he saw sagging and hanging, at the dustballs beneath the radiator and in the two corners of the room he could see while prone, and at the two—only two—half-hour sessions of physical therapy they allotted him daily. He demanded they not only sweep away the damn dustballs—the place was supposed to be spotless, for chrissakes, and cost enough, for chrissakes, that he should be able to eat off the floors—but also up his regimen of physical therapy to four times a day and even more—for chrissakes, he was a workingman with a mortgage and bills to pay. And he won out, the therapists came to love his against-all-odds attitude and determination, and almost six weeks after he was first brought in they watched him hobble away on crutches, walking solely on the balls of his feet and raising and lowering each foot as though he were fighting the suction of quicksand or had thirty-pound weights on each ankle. A few months later Sharon was still driving him to outpatient PT three times a week, and

Dan realized that he wasn't making much progress and perhaps never would, and that maybe he should consider the fact that he wasn't dead or paraplegic something of a miracle.

But he could never quite see it that way. He'd lost his truck, and the insurance on it was less than what it was worth to him, because it was worth everything; and they'd had to return the sale money on the destroyed camper, and he knew there wasn't a construction company in the world that would take a chance on hiring him now to so much as pound a nail in a wall, not with him having to use crutches or two canes except when standing still, and even when doing that his legs sometimes collapsing without warning, just literally letting him down. He hadn't been working steadily before the accident and didn't have workmen's comp, and despite selling the snowplow and small backhoe and some of his most valued tools, he was still owing on medical charges on top of the mortgage and other bills, never mind groceries and gas for Sharon's car, which needed a tune-up and oil change sometime soon. Between Sharon's paycheck from the one-stop shopping center where she worked as a cashier in the groceries department and the pittance sent to him by the state for having been permanently disabled, Evans was at the end of his tether at not being able—and seeing he'd never be able—to make ends meet. So he called Oldman, for who in town wouldn't, Oldman knowing not only about capuchins and the Second World War and split-rail fencing and useless ponies (among other critters) and photography and anything that had to do with town gossip and news, but also being the fairest and probably most rational person around, having a reputation for being, unofficially, the community's psychologist, ombudsman, local historian, and the one person just about everyone consulted if they needed something resolved that they couldn't figure.

And so Dan Evans called Oldman and told him that he was beyond broke, that although he wasn't a man who believed in suing his neighbors, there was, after all, the matter of that hitch that had cracked — the state police had taken photos at the site and, later, in the junkyard where the wrecked pickup had been towed, Sharon at Dan's behest had done the same — and he figured, yes, his condition was partly his fault as he hadn't secured his seat belt, but there was no law against driving without one and even if he had been wearing it that hitch shouldn't have split in two. He'd written to the company that manufactured the hitch and sent duplicate photos of what that broken hitch looked like, but the company hadn't responded in writing and wouldn't even tell him over the phone whether his letter and photos had been received. He didn't have money to hire a lawyer who could advise him as to whether he did or didn't have a case, but by god if he had the dough he'd sure spend it as foolishly as necessary to find out. Oldman went to Duncan, whom he knew peripherally at that time and because of Claire, and Duncan said he'd take on Dan's case, no questions asked as to payment, and whatever settlement he quite quickly wrung from that hitch manufacturer kept Dan and Sharon Evans in their home and saw them clear enough to even put some money into their bank account. Dan thereafter told Oldman that he'd offered to put more than chump change into Duncan's pockets for his services, but, to his incredulity, Duncan refused, telling him to put the money aside for what he would wish for the Evans couple to be a very long life, or at least for some unexpected rainy day. As if, Dan went on, any day could be rainier than the one that had broken his neck.

That was years back, but only last week Evans, Oldman told Duncan as they were eating the sandwiches and having a beer in Duncan's office, had called him because the neighbor's dog, Butler, which spent as much or more time with Dan as with its owners, had been, as usual, with Dan in the yard. Dan was managing without the two canes but was wrestling with his balance while trying to cover a pile of stacked cordwood with a heavy piece of tarpaulin when a UPS truck pulled into his drive. Without giving it a thought, Dan—walking on the balls of his feet in that infant-like gait he'd been hobbled with and swaying unsteadily—met the driver, who had hopped out of his truck with a package and waited on him. Butler was at Dan's side as usual, and after the UPS driver said, Hi, Dan Evans, right? and Dan replied, That's me, the driver started to hand Dan the package but Butler got between them and, in a most protective manner, latched on to the driver's hand. Dan grabbed Butler by the scruff of his neck, hollered for Sharon, and fell, at which point Butler let go and began to lick Dan's face. The UPS driver was not amused: he'd been bitten hard, and Sharon had to drive him to the emergency room; the man had to put in a call to UPS to explain that not only did the company have to retrieve the truck in the Evanses' drive but he also wanted UPS to back him in making a formal complaint to the proper authorities—and, Oldman said, believe me, he meant every authority—because he wanted that dog put down. Sharon tried to explain to the driver that in some odd way Dan, being partially crippled, really depended on the neighbor's dog, but the man wasn't listening and wasn't sympathetic; the mutt had drawn blood and he didn't give a damn whose dog it was, and maybe people like her husband who couldn't stand on his own two feet or walk straight shouldn't have any dog at all, given he'd sure proved he couldn't control the one he or their neighbor had.

So Oldman had had to make a number of visits a few days

after the incident, first to the local UPS office, where he knew the manager, then to the ASPCA—where Butler had been impounded and awaited sentencing—where he knew everyone, then to the town police who had taken in the driver's complaint but had already tabled it because the local UPS office manager had already seen to that, then back to the UPS office the next day, where he reasoned with the bitten UPS driver and got him to allow that any dog—including even golden retrievers, which are the happiest and friendliest of canines—might not understand that a stranger who makes a motion toward someone who's incapacitated isn't necessarily threatening but sure might be, and that, given Dan Evans's condition, he pretty much needed that dog around because he wasn't necessarily going to be able to take care of himself if something precarious should take place. And Oldman got the driver to agree, at least in some fashion, that if he were in Dan's position, he'd most likely appreciate a dog like that—

And then June knocked and entered. Oldman paused in midsentence, not because he was circumspect—which he was—but because he'd also turned to see who was interrupting his tale and felt a punch to his heart, his chest constricting for a split second before reason took over: the girl's face set him back almost thirty years before he returned to the moment, the present, and a world in which he knew there was always the possibility that everyone—this had been a popular theory in his youth—had a double. At which point Duncan looked at his watch and said, June, hello—god, I lost track of time—let me clear the desk, pull up a chair. But Oldman was already on his feet and sliding an armchair across the floor for her, and when she settled into it Duncan introduced them. And because Oldman's name as pronounced rhymed with *Holden,* June misheard and thought Holden was his name until Oldman at some later time corrected her misconception, explaining that his parents had given him, an only child, this odd nomenclature either because his mother—this was her version—wanted him to live to be an old man or because his father—this, his father's version—knew that his son would be called Old Man Smith when he reached his dotage, no matter whether his name were Vincent or Jonathan or Ebenezer or anything other than Oldman, so why not let the boy get used to the inevitable from the start. Having cleared his desk quickly and having nodded to Oldman to stay, Duncan relaxed back in his chair, but before he could ask how she and the baby were doing, how things were going, June placed twenty-five dollars on his desk and said: I believe this is yours.

No, he corrected her, it's yours. Sorry if I didn't make that clear. Iris wanted you to have something to tide you over for the week in case you needed it. And this—he reached into a drawer and pulled out an envelope, slid it across the desk—is for next week. If you can't make ends meet, you're to let me know: Iris doesn't want to be bothered by the details.

June colored slightly, adjusted the baby on her lap, undid the carrying blanket and unbuttoned the baby's sweater only to reveal another, both worn over a corduroy jumper. Luke's feet were roundly bundled, balled up in knitted socks. She too, Duncan figured, must have on two sweaters, as she wasn't wearing a jacket or scarf despite the deep chill. She didn't touch the cash or the envelope, shook her head, looked at him confusedly. I shouldn't be taking her money, she told him.

And why is that.

I'm not exactly earning it.

You don't have to. That wasn't a stipulation.

A—?

A requirement. You don't have to help Iris with anything, unless she asks. Which, I take it, she hasn't.

The only thing she's told me to do is bring Luke over every morning from ten to eleven.

Over?

Into her house.

Huh, Duncan said, now *that's* interesting. And what do you do when you're there?

Nothing. She holds Luke and talks and plays with him while I watch.

Really?

Yes.

And that's all?

June shrugged. I guess, she said. I mean, she doesn't talk to me, just gives Luke back when the hour is over.

Huh, Duncan repeated. Added, after a moment: Well, then, it's not as if she hasn't found something for you to do.

I can't understand why she'd pay for—

Look, you knew you might not have to do anything—

I was hoping—

Don't. Just take the envelope, and the money.

But I don't need it, not this week, there's still plenty of food—

You need warmer clothes, Duncan told her gruffly, and so does that baby. Winters are rough here. And long. It snows, usually a lot. If you want to do something for Iris, get yourself a pair of warm boots and a parka and some gloves so you'll be able to shovel snow. She won't ask you to, but you should clear the path from her place to the shed, then clear your own, so you can get wood for the fireplaces. And shovel a path around to the outside door and to the street, so that you can get out and I can bring in whatever Iris needs. She'll appreciate that.

Anybody'd appreciate that, Oldman agreed, turning to her, again feeling his chest constrict and again fighting its tightness. Besides, he continued, the days when you could hire a neighborhood kid to shovel your drive or sidewalk for a couple of bucks are over, and anyway we're talking about *Iris*—Oldman knew this because Duncan had confided in him, knowing that Oldman, being circumspect, being Oldman, wouldn't breathe a word about the girl's presence to Claire or to anyone in town—who hasn't allowed anyone, with few exceptions, to come onto her property for years and years. You should be very pleased to be on Iris's very short list of privileged people.

I'm not sure she wants me on that list.

Well, you're on it, Duncan told her. And then tells her that the money she receives isn't for groceries, that Iris leaves a list of what she needs in an envelope taped to the outer door on Wednesday evenings, and that June should do the same; Duncan leaves the delivery at the door on Thursday mornings. Otherwise, the money is June's to spend or save as she sees fit. Also, as there's no phone in the cottage and Iris doesn't want one put in, June is welcome to use Duncan's office phone if she wants or needs to. And she's to let him, not Iris, know if anything needs to be fixed in the cottage; again, Iris doesn't want to be bothered with such. And, of course, June is to come by on Fridays at three o'clock. Any questions? he asked.

June shook her head.

So take the money, he told her, and the envelope. Downtown shops are open until six except on Thursdays, when they're open until nine. There's also a big shopping center at the other end of town that's open seven days a week until ten at night except on Sundays, when it closes at eight.

Is there a bus?

The same one you took coming here.

Funny, Oldman mused aloud, I was planning on going over there myself, so I can offer you a lift and drop you at Iris's place on my way home.

I don't want to put you out—

You won't. I'd be glad to have the company, unless you've got other obligations, Oldman replied, and Duncan had to stop himself from grinning; June knew no one other than Iris and Duncan and was living within the confines of Iris's world and so couldn't possibly have other obligations, never mind plans, unless it was to walk the streets and gaze in the windows—Duncan was certain June wouldn't step foot into a shop, not yet, she'd first have to overcome her shyness, that innate discomfort that arose from some deep-rooted sense of inadequacy, neither of which she was shedding at that moment in his office. But it wasn't even Oldman's considerate suggestion that the girl, like any girl, might have something else (never mind something better) to do that made Duncan suppress a grin: it's that Oldman, as everyone in town knew, had gone out of his way to avoid that shopping center he'd long detested before it even opened because he understood that it would decimate the small stores and shops in town, empty the streets of shoppers, signal the death of downtown Thursday nights when just about everyone came out to make their purchases or perambulate or gallivant and gossip. No, Oldman didn't give a damn about the shopping center's long hours and cutthroat prices, its one-stop-for-everything-you-need convenience (from automotive supplies to clothes to hardware and fishing tackle, household goods, groceries), or the free parking provided for more vehicles than would ever fill its lot. Worse, Oldman was known to fume, even if that shopping center didn't drive the last nail into downtown's coffin, it served as the harbinger of things to come—some of which had already arrived—in the shape of those malls that were springing up, sprawling off the highways, with their restaurants, walking areas, recreational facilities. And Oldman was right, of course: some stores in and around the center of town had closed and, while not boarded up, sat behind empty, unwashed display windows; some once-established places made do with becoming secondhand clothing and furniture stores; and others—such as the pharmacy and the Puritan restaurant, the magazine-and-newspaper store, the diners, a pizza parlor, and a few bars—managed to remain as they were, along with the local newspaper building and town hall and police department, and those street-level offices whose shingles belonged to the town's doctors, accountants and lawyers, some of whom, like Duncan, lived above their offices and so kept the main street from being utterly deserted of foot traffic.

At any rate, Duncan, repressing that grin, said, I'd take Oldman up on that offer if I were you, and he picked up the envelope and put the twenty-five dollars into it and handed it to June, who, still hesitant, finally took it and thanked him, and to Oldman said: I really wouldn't want to trouble you.

It's no trouble at all, Oldman told her. In fact, it'd be a pleasure.

But before they reached the door, Duncan asked: And what about that shaggy dog story you were telling?

Butler was finally pardoned, came Oldman's reply, by the UPS guy himself, whom everyone convinced that the dog just decided for itself what its job is, which is to make sure no one does any more damage to Evans than what he already has to deal with.

Don't tell me he brought bones by Evans's place as an act of forgiveness.

Okay, Oldman laughed, I won't.

And Oldman ushered June and Luke onto the sidewalk and into the spotless Studebaker parked just outside Duncan's office, Duncan wondering how in the world Oldman managed to keep it running after all these years, wondering too how long it would take before June realized that he—Oldman—had taken her and that baby under his wing, had committed himself to them. The irony of it, Duncan reflected: first Claire, now June, both ostensibly under Iris's watch but Iris permanently self-discharged from duty. Not that Oldman would mention Iris, or Claire; Oldman was prudent. And patient, so he had a way of getting people to talk, and Duncan had no doubt that the girl would become comfortable with him—as comfortable, perhaps, as she could be with anyone—and maybe even, eventually, tell him about herself, without Oldman ever asking as to how she had come to be living at Iris's and never once mentioning the oddity of it. No, Oldman wouldn't pry, Duncan knew. He'd act as though there were no reason in the world why June shouldn't have ended up here, and he'd allow her to come to the conclusion that it was perfectly natural that he, Oldman, would be the one to take her best interests and the best interests of that baby to heart. Which he had already done, either because he'd seen something in her that no one else had ever noticed and might never, or because Oldman was doing what he always did, taking in strays—who could forget those feral monkeys, or the way Oldman pastured until it died an unbroken, useless, evil-tempered cow-kicking pony, or that string of mutts that seemingly came from nowhere and simply took up, each in turn, residence with him. And who could forget Claire, to whom he had been both mentor and, in his way, godfather. Why Oldman never married was a mystery to Duncan, for he must have been considered a fine catch for most women, being a steady, thoughtful, intelligent man—a farmer's son who loved working the land, a former war photographer, currently a semiretired newspaper darkroom manager, and for a generation and more the town's full-time confessor, shrink, adjudicator, adviser, unofficial lawman—who, now in his sixties, remained the area's most unapologetic, enduring bachelor. Duncan finished his beer, thinking that Oldman would make it through to a hundred, being who he was, and that before he got any older he'd see to it that June didn't leave that shopping center he so despised and had himself never stepped foot in without making sure she bought some proper clothes for the hard season to come; he'd help her select the warmest boots and gloves and caps, he'd make sure she and that baby had more than just a change of clothes, and he'd drive them to Iris's and make an arrangement to pick her up next Friday and every Friday thereafter—obviating the necessity of her walking to the bus stop with Luke in her arms—and bring her to Duncan's office.

And Duncan knew that early next week, at some moment or other, Oldman would walk in with breakfast or lunch for the two of them in hand and tell Duncan how he'd taken her shopping and afterward made a detour so that he could show her more than just the downtown and a shopping center. That he'd taken her to the port so she could see the fish-canning factories and the mills—shuttered, closed but for the ground floors that now served as outlet stores for woolen goods, although there was also a futureless cigar factory yet in operation — with their central watchtower and a granite-lined canal that had once coursed from the river and turned the great waterwheels that were no longer intact and were barely recognizable as such, being a tangle of yawping, dilapidated spokes and paddles precariously askew. And he'd tell Duncan he'd shown her the mill workers' apartments as well, old three-story buildings that had been carefully constructed with the same bricks in the same color as the mills, Oldman explaining to her that in the last century the corporation that had created the mills had also put up the workers' housing to match, then giving her a lesson in what Oldman considered to be regal Victorian industrial architecture whose grandeur had clearly outlasted the factories' usefulness. And he'd relate to Duncan how she'd taken everything in, the wrought-iron gates, the cobblestone streets that rimmed the factories, the granite sidewalks still extant on the backsides of the workers' apartments with their porches painted the same shade of gray as they'd originally been. He'd explained that the apartments were now rental units in which lived the elderly in their majority, people whose parents and grandparents had lived in the same apartments and spent their lifetimes working in the mills, and that most of these elderly inhabitants had also worked in them and had held on to those jobs until the end, which came mostly in the fifties. He'd also described to her the company stores, the ragmen and icemen who came in horse-drawn carts to collect old clothes and bedding and to supply ice for iceboxes, the best of which were oak and lined with tin. He'd told her that the mill workers first came from farms and hamlets far and wide, and later as immigrants from abroad, and that they'd had a quality of life they might not otherwise have had, never mind imagined, given they had work and apartments with indoor plumbing and cookstoves and iceboxes, and a company store that gave them credit on everything from clothes and shoes to dry goods and staples. He'd tell Duncan how she'd remained silent, just gazing at the buildings and taking in what he was saying, and that it was a given she'd never seen anything like those great docks rimming the riverfront or those mills and factories or that canal, never mind a town mostly built of brick and stone despite the abundance of trees, of wood, everywhere. So that Oldman had explained—June still wordless, the baby quiet on her lap—that timber never would have done, for while it was true that most houses outside of town were built of wood—some of them were upward of a hundred years old and most of them had never burned down—the factory owners and original town fathers wouldn't have taken such a chance on the town going up in flames. And he'd recount to Duncan that the only pleasure he'd taken from stepping foot inside that shopping center was the fact that it was obvious, given June's bewilderment, that she'd never stepped foot inside one either.

Oldman was the one to strap Luke into the carriage seat of the shopping cart. And despite his intense dislike of the place, he was in turn delighted and sorrowful at how overwhelmed—indeed, cowed—by the magnitude of the place she was, what with a dozen checkout stations neatly placed at the store's entrance and queues of shoppers and beyond them the expanse of endless aisles stocked to the brim, departments for baby clothes and toys, for footwear and hardware and automotive supplies, men's and women's casual and formal wear and outerwear and underwear, hunting and fishing outfits, even tackle—and in a separate area, with its own line of registers, groceries—as well as a food bar with counter and stools, where customers were ordering hamburgers and hotdogs and colas and coffee. Oldman explored the labyrinth haphazardly, the baby slapping happily at the shopping cart's rail, June wide-eyed beside him, clearly over-awed. In the baby department she finally opened the envelope and gave a small gasp, the color leaving her already wan face and she immobile, unable to gather her wits for a moment, turn-ing away and bringing a hand to her forehead. Oldman later told Duncan that he knew then there wasn't too little money but more than she'd ever had. When she finally turned back to face Oldman, she looked anguished and confused, and said: I don't understand. So Oldman replied there wasn't much about money that required understanding, she just needed to spend it as it needed to be spent.

Which he saw to it she did, outfitting that baby and herself with what he advised they'd be needing maybe even tomorrow, and then, in the end—to his surprise—June asking someone stocking a table of sweaters if there was a knitting and sewing section, which there was, where she carefully selected skeins and knitting and crocheting needles and woolen cloth and a sewing kit. She had more than enough money at the register, Oldman holding the baby until she paid and the items were packaged, and then he handed her the infant and carried her purchases to the Studebaker. Once they were on their way, figuring she might be hungry, he'd asked if she'd like some fried clams, add-ing that the Puritan had the best ever—and seeing it was about dinnertime anyway and how he was a bit hungry himself, that he'd appreciate her company. Whether because she was hun-gry or because she felt obliged—Oldman told Duncan that not since the war had he encountered anyone so passive, so emotion-ally flat, so apparently deadened by constant distress, and that he couldn't help thinking she'd survived something for reasons she couldn't understand and certainly didn't give herself credit for and, moreover, maybe hadn't even wanted to survive — June finally said, well, only if she, they, weren't inconveniencing him any more than she, they, already had.

The Puritan's interior had a warm glow, its booths covered with reddish-maroon faux leather, and the place was as yet uncrowded. Those who saw Oldman waved or said hello in greeting, and he knew they'd be wondering who the girl and baby were and realized he hadn't thought about what he'd say about them if asked, decided to just tell anyone curious enough to bring the subject up that she was new in town and that he'd met her through Duncan. They sat in a booth and the waitress brought a highchair for Luke and the baby played with bits of a banana June requested for him before they ordered. When Oldman asked what she'd like, June said she'd have the same as he was getting for himself, so he requested what he always did, a platter of fried belly clams with French fries, and by the time the food arrived he was telling June how the old-timers here still went clamming, how clamming was done. She ate slowly, like someone who hadn't seen food for a very long time and feared dying from ingesting it, and Oldman recounted to Duncan that she eventually announced that she'd never eaten clams before, hadn't even known what they might look like cooked. What he didn't tell Duncan, or anyone, and never would, was that as he watched June eat, the shock of déjà vu, though still unnerving, was making him marvel: the shape of her face, her thinness and height, her bone structure, her pallor, that peculiar opacity to her eyes — no glimpsing the soul through them — and the set of her mouth that suggested a resignation verging on vacuity, the shape of her hands, the way her shoulders sloped and hunched, the slowness with which she ate, were exactly those features and attributes of the one woman — or girl, for who knew how old she'd been—Oldman had utterly, inexplicably and improbably fallen in love with, in the midst of those horrible, and horrifying, circumstances at the end of the war, in a German town like so many hundreds that had been reduced to rubble by ruthlessly repetitive Allied bombings, its survivors a shocked, stunned, starving people—among them the homeless who had once resided there, surely also displaced persons, concentration camp survivors, freed POWs, the demobilized defeated—living in holes in the ground where cellars had been, or in buildings that had no fronts or sides, or in craters or beside mounds that had once been buildings, searching through the devastation for pieces of clothing, broken crockery, tintypes and spoons and forks and knives and pots and pans no matter their condition, something or anything they could patch together or cling to or use, and sifting through the dirt in what had once been streets or gardens or sidewalks for anything edible.

Oldman first saw her sitting in a fetal position on a rise of rubble, her head buried in her arms and her arms around her knees, her thin wrists and hands hanging limply from the sleeves of a man's tattered overcoat she'd somewhere found, in pants too short for her legs so that part of her shins and sockless ankles showed above the workman's boots she'd probably taken off the dead; he saw her in that position in those clothes, and from a distance of about twenty feet took the photograph—as was his job—that would be among tens of thousands taken of the war's destitute in a decimated land. Oldman took the photograph and she raised her head at the sound of the click, or maybe just raised her head, at any rate saw him and made an anguished, exhausted sound and held her hands up to signal *Don't* or *Stop,* and that second photograph he took—because it was too late to stop—was the only other he had of her, her face partially obscured and the overcoat listing over one of her stooped shoulders, revealing the filthy shirt—also a man's—she wore beneath it. He called out *Okay* and let the camera drop as he came closer, and she put her hands down. When he saw her face, a shock wave of certainty shot through him and he knew, simply knew, that this girl, this woman—she could have been sixteen or twenty-six, it was impossible to tell—was the one to whom his heart belonged. Would always.

Love at first sight.

He approached her with pity and pathos and a sudden desperation because of his abject certainty that he would lose her, for he was on the move with the army, and it was just a matter of days before the company to which he was attached would be gone; and as he approached her he suffered, for the first time in his life, the fear of loss, a terror of losing the one person he was meant to spend his life with, the one meant to be the mother of his children—although he didn't think this, since no words formed in his mind; there was simply a certainty coursing through him, releasing from the marrow of his bones—and he knew dread as he'd never known it before and would never know it since, for he was already mourning the loss of her in full knowledge that he'd be bereaved for the rest of his life; and Oldman determined to return and find her again as he warily, cautiously approached, never taking his eyes off her, finally stretching out his hand to stay her as he neared and took from his kit a fork and opened a can of rations and gave both into her hands, then crouched at her feet and watched her eat slowly, listlessly, hardly looking at the food but locking those pale expressionless eyes on his, finally handing him his fork and the can when half empty, wiping her mouth with a corner of that impossibly cavernous coat sleeve. He understood she couldn't eat more, that she had sense enough to realize she couldn't eat more because she hadn't eaten enough in weeks or even months to survive the shock to her system, she must have seen — as Oldman had — the starving devour food and die; but he handed her the can and fork back and spoke to her in English and then in pidgin French, the only French he knew, motioning for her to eat the rest later, but when she didn't react he stood and reached over and opened her coat and placed the can and fork on her lap, then closed the coat about her. Perhaps she was mute, or deaf, or didn't understand English or his terrible French — she could have been from anywhere neither language was spoken — so he pointed to himself and said *Oldman,* thereafter mouthing the syllables silently, ridiculously; and then he pointed to her, that mound on which she sat, and tried in sign language to tell her to stay there, to indicate he would return. But when he came back later that day, she was gone.

He saw her the next morning. He couldn't help but think, wanted to believe, that she was waiting for him. He had managed to requisition for himself an extra pair of military-issue socks, a scarf. He gave them to her, along with more rations. He found her every day over five days. On the third day he brought someone from the unit who spoke German to translate for him, but she remained mute and kept her empty eyes on Oldman and gave no indication that she either heard or understood what he had the man translate for him. Try giving her a pen and paper, the soldier told him; and the next day, along with the rations, Oldman handed her a piece of paper with his name and military address and also his home address on it, and although she pocketed the rations she seemed not to know to do the same with the paper, which she held in her hands without looking at it. Oldman folded and stuffed it into one of her outer pockets, then

gave her a pen and paper and motioned for her to write. She did
nothing, so he eventually took back the paper and put the pen
into that inner pocket of her coat. The last time he saw her, he
tried to show her that he was leaving but would return, pointing
to himself and walking his fingers through the air, then revers-
ing the direction and pointing at the ground where he stood.
He drew a heart with his hands, touched his fingers to his lips
and placed the kiss they held on her mouth as she studied him
passively. He finally spoke to her in a language he knew wasn't
hers, and maybe it was the seriousness in his voice or the desperation he knew to be on his face that made her come off that pile,
stand before him, place her palm on the hollow of his shoulder
as he reached beneath her open coat and touched her thin waist,
traced the bones of her hips. When she drew back, her opaque
eyes and her expression revealing nothing, she raised a hand to
her heart and tapped her chest.

She watched him go, Oldman turning back to see her standing there. He returned to the same spot several months later, on
furlough, still with the military and hitching rides or walking
interminable miles, knowing he didn't have much time and unsure as to how he would manage to bring her back to the States
but knowing he would find a way, do or die. But the rubble was
being cleared, streets were no longer a matter of paths winding
through the wreckage, people were passing stones hand to hand
and reconstructing houses, buildings, their lives; there were a
few shops, public wells, food relief stations, some temporary
shelters erected by the occupying forces. The heap upon which
she'd sat, where they'd met, was gone: there was nothing but an
open crossroad in its place. He had the photograph of her with
her hands up, her face only partially visible; he showed it to eve-

ryone he encountered, searched for her everywhere, and never found her, never saw her again.

After years passed he found he could no longer recall her face, not exactly, had only a vague impression of her because he'd made himself stop looking at, stop being haunted by, those two photographs he'd kept of her. When June walked into Duncan's office, there she was — no, not her, but such a likeness of her that he'd caught his breath, had had to gather his wits. And perhaps — for how could Oldman know; that girl, or woman, on that mound of rubble had never uttered a word — if she could have spoken, if she'd ever had, he told himself she'd have had June's low, soft voice, with its flat cadence, and June's way of speaking, with a quiet slowness that stemmed from shyness or a sense of inadequacy or perhaps her resolve to never be misunderstood — this last, Oldman would come to realize, was the crux of it, June having misunderstood in a heartbreaking manner the situation she'd gotten herself into and having no way of accurately deciphering the intentions of others — so that she measured every word, mostly said little, spoke plainly.

Oldman wasn't moved in the same way he'd been in his thirties and in a faraway land, but June's uncanny resemblance to the one love of his life — to whom he remained true — stirred his heart, awakened in him a panic he hadn't felt since being unable to find that girl, woman, who'd once sat solitary in the rubble of the war's aftermath. By the time introductions were made and June sat down with that baby on her lap, Oldman already knew he would do everything, anything, for her. He would never tell Duncan, or anyone, this, never reveal this even to June, who, upon finishing her meal and sitting across from him at the Puritan restaurant, put her hand to her heart and tapped her chest in that peculiar gesture of thanks he'd only once before witnessed. He will barely admit to himself and never say to Duncan, or to anyone, that he regretted—at that singular moment but not ever thereafter—that he was too old for love, and she too young.

1977

Sam

WHEN LEONARD CAME into the kitchen and said nonchalantly, You might consider taking some time off, it'd do you good, Sam suspected that Claire had spoken to the man. And shortly after Leonard left, there she was in his stead, having no right so far as Sam was concerned to enter his domain. Claire stood without saying a word, just leaned against the stainless steel counter not yet dry from being wiped down, silent and waiting and watching him, ignoring George altogether — the man was mopping with his back to them, working the same corner he'd been swishing that mop over, swaying over, for the last ten minutes. She folded her arms, remained without saying a word until Sam finally shook his head, then averted his gaze and went on about what he was doing, actually much of nothing — the pots and utensils were clean and hung, the dishes and trays cleaned and stacked, the glasses drying in the dishwasher — in order to avoid her eyes. She had,

Sam knew, a way of getting what she wanted not because she was argumentative or even insistent but because she was, at least from what he'd witnessed, unbelievably patient, impossibly present in an implausibly unobtrusive way. He knew Claire wasn't leaving, that she'd be there, leaning against that counter with her arms folded, waiting for him to speak when he finally finished doing what didn't need to be done. She'd stand there statuesque and motionless, although maybe she'd have crossed an ankle since he'd last looked, for as long as it took for him to acknowledge her, even if that meant the rest of the day or until hell froze over. So Sam wiped down both sinks and then the gleaming tiles behind them, finally folded and racked the dishrag and put both hands on the edge of a sink, hung his head and sighed before pushing off and turning around, then leaned back and mirrored her stance by folding his arms and an ankle and cocking his head.

No, he said.

That's probably the wrong answer to the wrong question.

Doesn't matter.

Of course it does.

Sam glanced over his shoulder, said: George, you're wearing that corner out, try stepping back some. Claire still didn't look at George, waited again for Sam to give her his full attention and he knew that she knew he couldn't put her off forever by commanding George to move a few feet back now and then and rewarding him with a nod whenever he found a new patch of floor to clean. George did as he was told, casting a grin over his shoulder, and began crooning *Jeepers Creepers, where'd ya get those peepers* in a croaky, off-key voice so low that anyone within range could only be thankful he could barely be heard. Sam looked at the ceiling and closed his eyes, shook his head, faced her again and saw that Claire wasn't bothered: George never annoyed her, and Sam—despite his own recalcitrance—knew he also couldn't, that most likely no one ever could, exasperate or dismay or irritate this woman whose imperturbability was as confounding as it was incomprehensible.

So, Claire said, the question of the day is: Are you a good driver? And that caught Sam off-guard, for it meant she'd learned if not from Leonard then maybe from George—who rarely spoke in sentences that could be understood, his speech being as garbled as his mind, but then Claire had a way of making people intelligible, who knew how?—that Sam wasn't blind in the eye over which he always wore a patch that also covered his eyebrow and some of his scarred, dented cheekbone.

Well, some people say I am, and some say I'm not, he told her.

In that case, I'll chance it.

Chance what.

That you'll be fine behind the wheel.

He looked at his feet, back at her. I've said no, he said, and I don't know why you can't take me seriously, or why you don't have one of your friends—I mean, you must have friends—go with you to wherever it is you're going. Which, by the way, you haven't bothered mentioning.

I take you very seriously, Claire said after a long moment. I'll explain this much: I need to go back to where I am—was—from. I haven't been there since I left, when I was seventeen. I don't need a friend because friends assume they're privileged to pry. You and I don't claim to know each other, and that seems to suit us both. My guess is I can trust you to not ask questions. About anything. It's only a day's drive. Spend the night and then do what you want, stay for a while or, if you want to turn right around, I'll arrange to get you to the closest airport and a ticket back the day after we get there. All expenses paid.

Go alone, drive yourself.

I'm not any good at driving except on back country roads in the dark, at about twenty miles an hour, tops. With the high beams on.

But you have a license.

And a car. But I can't manage highways, and I'll need the car when I'm there.

For those back roads.

That's all there is, back where I'm from. Was.

That repeated *where I am — was — from, where I'm from. Was* echoed in Sam: she didn't say *home,* just as he hadn't when he returned to his parents' place after he recovered — that's what the staff at the military hospital said he'd done, recovered, although he found himself discharged without those blown-away pieces of bone and flesh he'd lost. He couldn't recognize himself — or at least not that part of his face, almost half, that was now scarred, deformed — in the mirror, and he was no longer who he'd been when he'd left. Claire had never asked him about the eyepatch, the pockmarks, those scars, the partial earlobe, hadn't ever queried whether his disfigurement had come about in an accident, a crash, or been caused by what Sam, as many but not enough others, came to see as a calamity of history; and he'd come to trust that she'd never inquire, in the same manner she trusted him not to ask questions about her. That *where I am — was — from* didn't leave him wondering what she meant; her meaning was, as always in his experience of her, exact, she'd never spoken to him with anything but the utmost precision, had never allowed herself to be misunderstood, never left herself open to interpretation, never left herself open. He pondered the situation, her request, acutely aware that she hadn't said *home,* and this affected him, she'd allowed him a glimpse into her psyche or soul, whatever it is that dwells within that outer human shell of skin he, she, wears. He mulled over what she'd said about friends, about not being friends, about being able to remain guarded with each other: he knows nothing about her, she has never told him or, to his knowledge, Leonard, certainly not George, or anyone within Sam's earshot anything personal, and it's a comfort to him that he doesn't know her history any more than she knows his, that she doesn't pry or, god forbid, talk about herself—Sam doesn't want to be subjected to the mania of someone else's story and sentiments, for he is, was forced to become, an expert at keeping his own story and emotions under wraps. And maybe, he considered, he and she were sufficiently alike, shy of intimacy and judgments; perhaps she, like Sam, long ago learned that it's easier to remain content with the superficial in human relations, to never violate the calm that lies upon the surface of things.

I have to talk to Leonard, he finally said.

I'll wait.

Don't, he told her.

See you tomorrow then, she replied gracefully, no tension in her expression, her voice, her stride as she left. He realized that the ease with which she handles herself should make him feel comfortable, but it doesn't. How awkward he might feel, being with her in a car for hours on end, being with her alone, bothered him: he lives a solitary existence when he isn't in Leonard's soup kitchen, where he's spent three years, more, listening to George at the end of the shift trying to carry the only tune he's ever sung in Sam's presence. And maybe he does need a break, Sam thought, maybe it'd be all right to leave George to himself mopping one of the corners rather than worrying him onto other parts of the floor or, as he did now, telling George to call it a day and taking the mop from his hands and then listening to his off-key singing fade as he left. Sam mopped methodically, found the work soothing, tried to convince himself he should indeed talk to Leonard, that Claire had always struck him as someone not so much aloof as self-contained, deft: yes, deft. He'd been impressed by the way she got the homeless and mad and addicted and sick and deformed—wasted, broken people, all of them down and out and not fitting in in one way or another, some in many ways, some in all—to talk to her as they lined up waiting for the kitchen to open, the way she listened to them, the way she let them convince themselves that they should allow her to photograph them, which they did. For she somehow made them feel worthy, unique, to be among the counted. He's spent a lot of time, on that break between cooking and serving, watching her work—Leonard having told him nothing about her except that she'd been a photojournalist who'd walked away from the job, and that she'd come to volunteer—as the toothless smile for her and the mad pause long enough to stare into her lens, the heroin addicts bringing their swollen, sore-infested hands to their faces and gazing at her with that faraway look in their jaundiced eyes, the sick unselfconsciously displaying their skeletal or obese frames, the deformed revealing their stumps or humps or scars, the homeless drawing themselves up to their full height with great pride or insolence despite how matted their hair, how filthy their clothes or skin. No matter, Sam had concluded some time ago, her reasons for photographing them—reasons he couldn't fathom, although he'd had to quell his suspicion that she might be preying on the gullible: he knew full well that people who have nothing are often the most credulous, the most given to delusion. But he'd suppressed his misgivings, hadn't judged her; after all, it seemed to him, her subjects, the men and women who came here to eat, became before her camera the human beings they'd once been and still were, capable—at least for that split second in which she captured their likeness on film—of the self-esteem, dignity, Claire gave them. To give that, he believed, she'd had to have found them blameless to some degree for what had befallen them, or at least seen something other than shame in their condition, which condition they willingly bared before her camera, allowed her to record.

Yes, she was deft, deft also behind the counter as she filled their plates, seeing to it that each got no more or less than another. Claire didn't have to be told to stay out of Sam's way, knew without asking what needed to be done from the start, Leonard announcing before lunch one day that she'd be an addition on the line—Sam fumed at the short notice, thinking things wouldn't go smoothly—and there she was, as though she'd been born to the work, knowing which pans needed refilling and when, which utensils to use, watching that the line moved and that everyone was able to carry their trays and find a seat without incident, without rubbing elbows. She asked no questions, didn't chatter, didn't joke, and never once commented on George being uselessly everywhere underfoot with that mop and his constant, croaked crooning of the one refrain he'd ever learned or remembered.

Jeepers Creepers: six days a week, with Saturdays going long, those three and more years. Hell, Sam thought, why not talk to Leonard.

The way Sam saw it, Leonard was more than just a decent man who put out food for those who hadn't eaten, who couldn't afford to eat: he was someone Sam credited with saving his life, not that Leonard ever knew. Though maybe Leonard suspected Sam faced empty nights that sometimes still held those terrors which were—when he first came out of the hospital and spent two months at home before moving into Freddie's—constant and incomprehensible to his parents, with whom he couldn't speak, his mother always crying at the sight of him, his father stiffbacked and proper and acting as though nothing at all had happened, as though his son hadn't been maimed, disfigured and somewhat deranged by what he'd seen and what he'd done, what he'd finally suffered in Nam. Sam refused to see aunts, uncles, cousins, either of the two girls from high school to whom he'd written and who'd written in return during his tour of duty, and that worsened his home situation, what with his mother unable to hold back her emotions at the sight of him, of what had become of him, and his father impatient with what he considered unmanliness, remarking that everyone had a cross to bear and that Sam should be grateful to have survived and proud to have served his country and now needed to get on with his life. Eventually Sam simply locked himself in his room, leaving it only after his parents were asleep but never setting foot outside the house even then, until Sam's brother, older by a decade, managed to get him to open his door and found beyond the clutter the shadow of his brother, who hadn't cut his hair or shaved and smelled as though he hadn't bathed, and said: If you can't live with them, leave.

And so Sam showed up with a duffel bag on Freddie's Lower East Side stoop one midnight and rang his bell, got buzzed in, and walked as many stairs as he had to before coming to Freddie's open door. Jesus, Freddie said, they really messed you up, man, come on in. And then showed Sam the couch, which he crashed on for what turned out to be the longest temporary arrangement he or Freddie had ever known. Freddie didn't ask questions, let Sam withdraw, didn't prompt him to go out, didn't complain that Sam spent aphasic hours just sitting on that couch with his arms around his knees and his heels on the cushions, staring at the peeling walls, at the flakes from the ceiling that littered the floor. Freddie, with that peace symbol tattooed above his ankle and beads around his neck, came and went, played pickup basketball games on the neighborhood's courts, bought groceries, did the cooking and laundry, did his drug dealing in other boroughs, and never asked Sam for money. He didn't leave his bedroom until late afternoon whenever Gloria stayed over—she rarely arrived on weeknights, came mostly on weekends and was sometimes accompanied by crazy Rita, lovely Rita, who unabashedly that first time she found Sam there made him move over after Gloria and Freddie had gone to bed and pulled out the couch Sam hadn't even realized was a convertible, then stretched out and slept on it, breathing like a baby, not making a sound and not stirring while Sam fretted, sat on the mattress edge, went sleepless. And Freddie always started the day with a sampling of what he was dealing or keeping for himself, Freddie always generous with whatever drugs he had on hand and Sam partaking gratis until he was able to contribute a bit of cash, which was after Sam's brother managed to get him to a shrink who was more than willing—Sam never knew what the man owed Sam's brother—to certify he was incapable of holding down a job. That brought in welfare and food stamps, which, as Freddie pointed out, finally got Sam out of the apartment, once for the appointment and then for the once-monthly journey around the corner to the check-cashing joint.

They'd met in Danang, swimmers at dawn in the South China Sea who afterward homed in on each other and sat in their skivvies at the shore's edge complaining of the relentless heat, the ants, the rats, the jungle, the impossibility of knowing who the enemy was if not everyone. Freddie told Sam that the mission, whatever it was, in Nam was insane, that he'd spent his first weeks at Saigon's airport unloading the dead in body bags and freaking out at what the future obviously held for him. That when he learned of tryouts for a general's basketball team — The fucking idiots have *teams,* can you believe it, oh let us not go without some good old-fashioned, red-blooded amusement in this lovely country, Freddie quipped — he saw his only chance at salvation. He'd played ball in Alphabet City and at the Cage on West 4th with the best nonpro guys in the universe, and when he tried out for the team he knew he was playing for his life. At five-eight and 150 pounds, Freddie gave better than he got on court during the tryout, backing into and racing around guys who were almost a foot taller and a lot heavier than he was and confounding them with his moves, shooting over their heads; and he was perfect from the foul line. Back in the city, Freddie told him, he'd practiced making nine out of ten shots from half-court, spent a lot of time perfecting that because — given his size — fearlessness and quickness and great hands only counted for so much.

He made the team, was playing his way through the war, and he got Sam to talking and later took him drinking at hooker bars where the girls, who were always pimped and usually by their brothers, weren't so mercenary as those in Saigon, Freddie told him, offering to pay for two girls; but Sam admitted that he couldn't imagine intimacy with anyone who looked exactly like everyone else who was trying to kill him. Freddie sympathized, said, Well, no hard feelings, and the friendship they struck up survived that and their time together, and they kept in touch after Freddie got out, Sam writing to him what he couldn't to his parents and brother or those two girls from high school, to hell with the censors, and at the bitter end of his tour of duty, with half his face and some of his upper body blown to bits, he'd gotten a letter from Freddie with his address and phone number and an open invitation to come by whenever he got home, that he had a small pad and knew some crazy chicks and where to get the best of everything that Nam, Mexico and Jamaica had to offer, that life was good and the good life was what anyone who'd seen action and survived it could surely use. For the transition could be rough.

It was. There had been no debriefing. No one at the hospital could or even thought to tell Sam how he might get on with his life looking the way he did; they considered him fortunate to be alive and not to have lost that left eye, whose shape now bore no resemblance to the other eye's and whose lid would remain scaly. Neither doctors nor nurses flinched at the sight of him, they'd seen worse than eviscerated earlobes, cheekbones that couldn't be put back together again, shrapnel scarring, missing shoulder and chest flesh. Sam's leaving the hospital consisted of nothing more than being handed his pay and discharge papers and being accompanied to the door, and once outside he found that eyepatch counted for little, for it didn't cover enough: people gasped, or stared, or turned away at the sight of him. Which sight left his mother weeping, his father pretending nothing had changed.

But everything had. When Freddie and Gloria and crazy, lovely Rita finally got Sam—who'd crashed on Freddie's couch for more than a year by then—to finally leave the apartment with them, at least after dark, he found himself in a deteriorated, deteriorating neighborhood rife with runaway kids and ex-cons and lunatics and dropouts and bums and alcoholics and addicts, hookers and pimps who owned the streets after store-front grates were lowered and locked as night rolled in, every-one nocturnal and drifting or claiming a piece of turf that oth-ers sometimes safely and sometimes not wandered in and out of. The Lower East Side, the East Village, Alphabet City, were crawling with broken people lounging on broken stoops, un-abashedly humping in the alleyways and parks, sleeping like the dead where they chose to or where they fell, everyone seemingly victimized by circumstances of their own creation as well as by one another or by strangers. The volume of trash was breath-taking, garbage cans overflowed or were kicked over, newspa-pers and takeout containers, oily paper bags and castaway fries and bones, beer cans and soda bottles littered the gutters. Every one of the night's denizens, to whom the dark streets belonged, hated the cops. Man, you should've been here a few years back for the good times, Freddie told him, the Age of Aquarius was something.

And maybe Sam would still have been there—sleeping on that couch, letting himself occasionally be guided into the nights and finally the daylight to walk through a tarnished world that left him wondering why he'd fought and what he'd fought for, letting hours become weeks, letting months and years pass, stay-ing safe, willfully dysfunctional, at times comatose—if Fred-die hadn't died. But his final drug deal went south, and al-though Freddie was gone—which spelled the end of Gloria and Rita, both simply melting back into wherever they'd sprung from—his ghost wasn't. Freddie's death and ghostly presence shocked Sam into straightening out to the extent he was capa-ble of, set him to call his brother, forced his retreat into a small tenement apartment in the West Village his brother—who was, ostensibly, happily married—to no one's knowledge, including Sam's, maintained for trysts he sometimes managed during those long executive lunches. Three conditions, his brother told Sam: keep the place spotless; don't ever be around between eleven and four, excepting weekends; and stop fucking living off the government.

His final welfare check and food stamps lasted him more than a month; after that, when he was down to small change, he joined the line at the soup kitchen. Leonard's place kept him from starving, but not from the humiliation he felt at being there; and maybe that's what Leonard, who at the time was behind the counter as well as overseeing the prep and cooking, noticed, for he quietly asked one day, Hey, soldier, are you living on the streets? Sam looked at him in surprise—he later pondered that Leonard must have surmised that Sam had been wounded in the war—and met Leonard's eye, shook his head, said, Nah, I'm all set. Well, if you're interested in working, come around and see me some afternoon after four, just knock, Leonard told him. Two days later, the way Sam saw it, Leonard saved Sam's life by giving him a job. You'll have to tie your hair back, Leonard cautioned, and shave off the beard, I need my kitchen to meet regulations, and no one here is going to give a damn as to what you look like.

Most everyone cringes when they see me as it is, Sam replied, I'd scare people off if I did that.

Not my people, Leonard assured him.

And that was that: Leonard had Sam start by racking cups and dishes, filling silverware trays, putting bread on the tables, bussing, washing plates and trays and pots and pans, washing down counters, setting up for the next day, before he taught him how to handle a knife, to prep and cook for a multitude whose welfare Leonard kept foremost in mind. Sam eventually went on to take stock of inventory, plan the meals, oversee the kitchen and serving and volunteers. Leonard, a fair man, raised Sam's salary twice, never questioned him about anything personal, never told him anything about himself: Sam, after all this time, knows nothing about Leonard's personal life, whether he has a girlfriend or a wife or children, and although Sam can guess what the man's politics are—Republicans don't run soup kitchens or hire the likes of someone like Sam, even if he has shaved—he doesn't know how old Leonard is or how or why he runs a soup kitchen, or how he keeps it running smoothly despite what must be funding problems, which Leonard only occasionally hints at; what, if anything, Leonard manages to pay himself—after doling out what he considers paltry checks to those who aren't volunteers and for those incidentals such as paying off cops to turn a blind eye to the occasional disturbance that occurs in the sidewalk lineup, never mind occasionally bailing out of jail one or another of the kitchen's regulars—is a mystery Sam hasn't solved.

So, Leonard said, walking into the kitchen to find Sam with a faraway look on his face, leaning on the wrung mop.

Hey, Sam rejoined.

Where's George?

I sent him off.

That tune get to you?

His singing did.

Leonard smiled. You might consider taking some time off, Sam, it'd do you good. And it's occurred to me that you're due a break.

I'm not asking for one.

I figured Claire might talk you into it.

Sam resisted the urge to ask what Claire had said to make Leonard as malleable, as willing to do her bidding, as the people she photographed while they stood in line to receive what was most likely their only meal of the day.

And anyway, I've been thinking, hell, I could really use a turn in the kitchen, I've been away from it too long. So take this, Leonard continued, reaching into a shirt pocket and handing Sam a check. It'll cover you for a couple of weeks.

It's not a done deal, Leonard. I mean, I'm still mulling it over.

Well, don't bother. We'll survive without you.

Sam looked at the check, shook his head, held it up in Leonard's direction. Is she paying for this?

That check, Leonard pronounced slowly, like every other I write, comes from common funds.

To which Claire contributes?

Has for a while. And, I assume, will continue to do so, no matter what you decide.

You assume.

Look, she's been very generous—

But if I don't—

She wouldn't turn her back on us, Sam. She isn't like that.

To tell you the truth, I don't know what she's like.

Then do me a favor, Leonard replied, cash the damn check, take a break, and find out.

Sam took a deep breath, two, and relented, said: Okay. He told himself he'd drive Claire to where she was, is, from, as a favor to Leonard, and he told Claire as he got behind the wheel of her car his only condition: No photographs. Of you, she clarified. Of me, came his response: he'd caught that appraising glance, her interest piqued by how much scarring the aviator sunglasses didn't cover—much less than the eyepatch he had in his shirt pocket—despite the blinder cut from suede on the left frame that kept anyone from seeing his deformed eye in profile. Deal, Claire pronounced. Traffic was light, the clutch caught high, the gears changed smoothly. Claire navigated, seldom consulting the map. He was aware that she'd turn her head to glance backward whenever he had to crane his neck to see what the blinder and side-view mirror didn't allow. He thought of telling her that he was used to driving with these glasses, with this blinder—being behind the wheel painfully reminding him of those day trips out of the city with Freddie, Gloria, Rita—but he didn't want to be asked questions, didn't want to remember what he couldn't help being reminded of, and was relieved when Claire eventually relaxed back into her seat, no longer mimed his glances to the rear, settled into a quietude she finally broke to direct him onto an interstate and instantly interrupted memories he couldn't stem. He merged into light traffic, broke his resolution to not attempt a conversation. So, he said, you only drive on back roads in the dark.

In the middle of the night, she affirmed, at a snail's pace.

Strange.

Purposeful, actually. The headlights capture deer and possums and raccoons, any nocturnal creatures, and while they stand stockstill they're sometimes even approachable because they're mesmerized, and there have been times when I've been able to open the door very quietly and ease toward them; often even the deer will remain motionless, statuesque, staring with eyes shining like refracted tinsel, shocked at being blinded by the light—no, not blinded exactly, just astonished by the unnatural, by this glare that's come out of nowhere—until I take the photo. The click of the shutter always sends them on their way, the deer bounding off and the raccoons scurrying and the possums waddling into the invisible, into that swamp of night beyond the road I can't penetrate.

And he didn't know how to carry on the conversation, didn't know how to carry on with her, not that he had to, for she'd already lapsed back into a silence that enveloped her, him. Which, he sensed, she used to protect herself, remain inviolable. He hadn't needed to adjust his seat before setting off; whoever had last been behind the wheel was Sam's height, most likely a friend, someone Claire didn't trust to not ask questions as to where they were going and why, as to what her childhood had been like, when and how she'd walked away from the place she was from, whom she'd left behind, what she might face upon this returning. She trusted—in a sense, charged—him to remain unfamiliar, to ask nothing; and so he contemplated her strangeness, her seriousness, the pointed effortlessness with which she spoke—that deftness again—that made him consider the way she searched out creatures in the dead of night, made him see them through her eyes, and then—having said all she wanted to—cloaked herself in silence. She was unlike any woman he'd known: unlike his mother, who couldn't stand to see him the way he was, unwhole and unlike who he'd been; unlike the girls in high school, given to hormonal madness and extreme silliness; unlike the bar girls in Danang, with whom every soldier who chose to had, for a start, a pecuniary relationship, paying for their drinks or paying for them to sit or dance with them, maybe later paying them for sex, none of the girls caring who chose to pay for this or that or the other. Unlike, too, crazy, lovely Rita, making herself at home in Freddie's livingroom, which included Sam on that couch, a lava lamp on a three-legged stand, a huge TV console that Freddie had bought from the super, who, everyone knew, dealt in stolen goods; Rita shooing Sam from the couch and pulling it out and nice-as-you-please taking to the right side of the mattress and stretching out to sleep, unmindful of Sam sitting on the edge of the bed in a cold sweat, staring at the television, which he'd muted, going sleepless through the night because of her closeness, the delectability of her scent, the way she'd once said to him *Sam, show us your hands,* and he'd reacted as though given a military order, placed his hands in Rita's so that she and Gloria could examine them, Rita tracing the lines on his palms and saying to Gloria—they'd been talking about workingmen having manicures on Friday nights, wanting those calluses and broken fingernails to be smoothed, wanting to have soft hands with which to touch their dates, their wives—*Now this is what we're talking about, what woman wouldn't want these roving all over her.* She hadn't let go quickly enough, left him struggling against thinking of Rita in the way he hadn't thought of her before—he didn't want to come to life, he'd been content to be left to himself in that livingroom, he had no desire to rejoin the world, didn't want to desire anything or anyone—but breathing in the scent Rita left on those rumpled sheets, remembering the way she'd held his hands, made him realize how numb he'd become, and made him want to cry at the thought of what he might never be.

Eventually he learned to sleep next to her, trusting her to sleep. Which trust was broken one night when, caught in that netherworld between wake and sleep, trapped in transition, he felt her hand on his chest and stilled her, grabbed her wrist. They listened to each other breathe for what seemed an eternity to him before she tried to move her hand, and again he stopped her, held her wrist, whispered, Hey. Hey, Rita, I don't know about this. And she said, So what is it you don't know about, is it this?—and kissed him—or this?—and she ran her tongue along the side of his throat—or this?—and covered his thigh with hers. She was gentle, slow, and something in him caved, he gave up, gave in, gave himself over to her, and afterward as she slept he lay awake on the other side of that line he'd never before crossed, the one Rita had gotten him to trespass. And the next day she didn't act as though nothing had happened between them but wasn't any different than she always was—chattering and joking and laughing with Gloria in the kitchen, ribbing Freddie, ribbing Sam—except for the ease with which she now made Sam move over on the couch so she could recline, unabashedly let her legs drape over his thighs as though that were the most natural thing in the world, not claiming him but simply making herself comfortable, and he realized, letting one hand rest on her knee, that there had been nothing natural about him or his state of being for a very long time, that he'd broken through, been hauled through, the barrier that had kept him wrapped up in himself, the deformity of his face and shoulder and arm that would always remind him of what he wanted to forget. He realized he wasn't able to shed his skin, go back in time, forget what had happened except during those moments—which he came to crave—in which he could no longer tell where he began or ended, where she.

He didn't fall in love with her. But he loved her dusky skin, the astonishing softness of her, the way she smelled, tasted, the way she was: small-shouldered, small-breasted, with a waist he could place his hands around and almost touch his fingers, her backside taut, high, her legs and arms long-muscled, defined. He loved her voice, the shape of her ears, her touch, her patience, the slowness with which she pulled him out of himself and the steadfastness with which she slowly brought him out into the world, taking him by the hand and leading him onto the streets, protecting and navigating him through a spring and then a summer, into the autumn and beyond, making love to him in the flickering light of the mute television and removing that patch, kissing his damaged face, shoulder, arm, telling him the while, *Don't ever, ever think that you're not fine, you are perfect,* and meaning it, never mentioning love and not — ever — expecting him to mention it either; that wasn't in the cards and wouldn't have been even if she weren't married to someone she never alluded to — it was Gloria who once mentioned that Rita's husband was doing time in prison; at any rate, they didn't fall in love, speak of love. Nor did Sam ever thank her for having removed that eyepatch, having made him feel — for moments on end — that he was the same person he'd once thought himself to be.

Crazy, lovely, laughing, joking, chatterbox Rita, leading him onto the streets and through seasons and snuggling next to him in whatever jalopy Freddie managed to borrow — people always owed him money or favors — and them driving to the reservoirs and lakes and ponds Freddie knew, stopping for hotdogs and hamburgers or ice cream along the way to and from, parking next to breaks in fences that hemmed in state lands, bushwhacking through the woods or following paths he remembered. How Freddie knew these places he never said, but he always had a destination in mind, which they always reached, and on the edge of the reservoir or pond or lake, in some deserted place, he and Sam would strip out of their clothes and ease into the dark waters, gasp at the liquid freeze flowing over their bodies, the two of them swimming out into the deep, Freddie always in the lead but never too far ahead, never leaving Sam beyond reach and rescue, knowing Sam might at any moment suffer an irrepressible fear to do with his, their, vulnerability in these nowhere places, where of a sudden malevolence might erupt, take shape out of the forest or take hold of them from the liquid depths below. Sam tried over and again, when swimming with Freddie, to concentrate on the whiteness of his arms, the rhythm of his strokes and of his breathing, or on the sight of Rita and Gloria sunning themselves like lizards on the shore, gorgeously indifferent to and resplendent in their nudity, or simply on trailing in Freddie's wake, but he always lost out to paranoia, sooner or later found himself unable to continue because convinced of impending evil emanating from the woods, or because certain that the drowned were rising beneath him, their hands and mouths seeking to grab and suck at him, destroy him. When that certainty, that conviction, took hold, Sam would feel himself becoming paralyzed, begin fighting for breath, flail about, finally cry out: *Freddie, I'm freaking.*

Freddie never needed to hear anything more, and never asked what was wrong. He always herded Sam back to shore. He never questioned Sam's fixations, and neither of them ever mentioned how they'd met as equally strong swimmers in another world, never spoke of the South China Sea's jade-like opacity, never reminisced about the expanse of Danang's beach, the surf, the way people lived in huts and the way they could carry their lives in those buckets that hung from wooden yokes they placed on their shoulders, how beautiful the fishing boats with their prayer flags waving black and blood orange in the wind, the way there was no dawn and no dusk. Sam never recounted that he came to feel that all Vietnamese — those who fawned in pretended friendship, those who collaborated, those who lost everything, those who hadn't, those on the side of the U.S. fighting in support of the regime in the south — hated him, hated each and every American soldier, even those who had qualms, because they were part of a machine that emptied out and burned down villages, wiped them off the map. The machine dropped thousands of leaflets before strafing and bombing and burning—doing exactly what the leaflets warned they would, demolishing lives and livelihoods without a care as to whether anyone heeded printed commands that probably couldn't even be read, all those peasants and fisherfolk in their conical hats with their seminaked children and their animals dying or fleeing as their homes and the countryside smoldered, as the rice paddies were cratered and the levees leveled, the jungles eaten by flames, all to no effect. The decimation of what seemed to Sam to have been half of South Vietnam, the relocation of what seemed to him half its population, the pervasive missions to engage and kill what enemy they encountered—which enemy looked like everyone else, dressed in the same baggy pants and sandals or went barefoot like everyone else; you never knew whether some village elder or child walking toward you with a smile would toss a grenade—without taking one inch of territory, without securing one godforsaken square foot of earth, had only one effect and that was to shore up resistance. No, he and Freddie had only spoken of Nam in Danang and never mentioned the place afterward, no matter that Sam for so long had simulated catatonia on Freddie's livingroom couch, no matter that he couldn't manage to swim unencumbered of the past, no matter whether Freddie surmised or understood that Sam used his mutilated countenance to shield his worse-wounded psyche. For nothing either of them, or anyone, could say would bring back the dead, or disappear those wounds that couldn't be seen, the ones that suppurated in minds and souls and wouldn't heal.

Sam didn't want to think about all that went unsaid between him and Freddie, didn't want to think about Freddie or Gloria or Rita, didn't want to be reminded of the last time he drove, and now on the road with Claire cannot help but remember, again feels the blow he suffered when Freddie died; Claire's silence, the driving, has left Sam vulnerable, sorrow grips him, twists a fist into his solar plexus, pains him the way it did for months after Freddie was gone, and rather than weep—he is on the verge—Sam forces himself to concentrate on the broken lines that separate his from the passing lane, on the engine's sound, on the highway; at least this route isn't familiar, he's never been this far north, still can't believe he agreed to leave the soup kitchen behind without knowing where he was going, where he'd stay, frets that he's trusting this day and this evening and maybe tomorrow and the next two weeks to this woman who rides silently in the bucket seat next to him. It again strikes him hard that he has no idea of who she is, glances at her almost angrily; and although Claire doesn't appear to notice, she reaches for her camera, leans back, raises it, quickly points it at him. Before his hand comes off the wheel to ward her off, she turns and focuses through the windshield, adjusts the lens but doesn't click the shutter, simply keeps the camera to her eye. As though, he almost immediately comes to consider, to dismiss him.

They make one longish stop after the day is more than half gone, after they'd left the highway and were traveling secondary routes, Claire directing them through decaying mill towns, hamlets with the inevitable steepled church to one or the other side of the inevitable village green, seaside resorts whose arcades were already shuttered for the season. Inland, again, in a town that looked much like some they'd already passed through, she had Sam pull over and park before a bookstore he wouldn't likely have noticed, as it was housed in a home replete with col-

umns and porch and curtained windows, with only a small sign
in its door window that announced used and rare books. Once
inside, to Sam's surprise, Claire asked whether there were any
cookbooks; Sam had never consulted any, he'd learned what
he knew from Leonard in terms of preparing simple meals
for a hundred people a day, none of whom ever complained
about what was put on their plates. They were led to one of
the bookstore's niches, where Sam watched Claire peruse old
cookbooks, some of whose covers were leather, taking her time
looking through the contents of several before choosing *Good-
wife Mullen's Pilgrim Recipes*—a reprint dated 1894—and paying what Sam considered to be a small fortune for it. After it was
wrapped in brown paper and string, she carried it like a school-
girl, crooked in one arm, with that camera slung over a shoulder. In a restaurant just steps beyond the bookstore, she led Sam
to a back table and placed the book on her lap, the camera on
the table next to her.

The place was dimly lit. She regarded Sam intently as she
ate, as though she could see through those sunglasses he hadn't
removed, wouldn't dream of removing. He tried to not be un-
easy; his shades, he knew, were so dark she couldn't possibly see
that damaged, misshapen eye, but he avoided her gaze anyway
and concentrated on his food, the coffee, eventually the camera
on the table. You know, he remarked, you use that like a shield.

She paused in surprise, held her sandwich in midair, thought
for a moment. Not really, she countered, though it's true that
holding a camera to the eye changes your relationship to whatever's in front of you, you get to edit out everything except what
you're focused on, and that process creates a dissociation because you're not part of any picture. Also true: it's incredibly
liberating, because the camera is like a window between you

and anything taking place, and you're responsible for nothing except deciding when or whether to press the shutter button. Every photographer I know admits that the act of photographing allows them to witness what at times they'd otherwise turn away from if they didn't have a camera between them and what they're seeing. When I'm looking through that viewfinder, I feel like I've been granted absolution, that I've granted myself absolution, that I'm no longer quite human. I might suffer what everyone else in the world does—loneliness, unrequited love, regrets—or be the happiest of sentimental slobs, but the moment I focus a lens, choose what to frame, I'm utterly freed from both past and future because I'm caught up in an instant that will never have either as soon as that shutter is pressed. I feel absolutely nothing when that happens, and when it's over, I just want to repeat that perfect sensation of separation, of power, for at least a split second. This camera, she continued thoughtfully, is my addiction. Those shades—she gestured with her sandwich—and that eyepatch: *those* are shields.

When he didn't respond—she'd turned the tables on him, and she wasn't wrong—she smiled at him, and they finished lunch without speaking and returned to the car, continued wordlessly on. Her silence bothered him because it somehow beguiled—she wasn't, he again realized, like any woman he'd ever known, she had no need to chat or banter or, like his mother, those high school girls, Gloria and Rita, annoyingly ask what he was thinking, a question that so infringed on what he considered to be the privacy of his thoughts that most of the time he replied he wasn't thinking anything at all. Her silence chafed, but intrigued: it was all he could do to keep his mind on the driving, wondering as he did where they were going, when they would arrive, what arrangements had been made, why—while she'd made clear she didn't want to be questioned — Claire trusted him to respect her wishes, ask nothing of her.

They headed back toward the coast, and when they finally swung on to an old highway that paralleled it, the sun was low, leaden, the light diffuse. He'd never encountered such a landscape, bog and marshland and forest stretching infinite from one side of the road, on the opposite the ocean heaving below cliffs and promontories, breaking upon rocky beaches and sandy coves and beyond dunes that sometimes allowed no more than a glimpse of the water's distant horizon. Nothing was familiar, nothing evocative of his past, and although still somewhat unnerved, beguiled, bothered, Sam also felt relieved to suddenly realize that his past had stopped erupting, his memories kept at bay. Claire rolled her window down at that moment — the rush of air was bracing — and surprisingly mused aloud, as if she had read his mind, Reminiscence is such a curious thing: I know this place like the back of my hand, I can conjure at will every curve of this road, every dune and cliff and cove, but what I can never recall is the way the world here smells; that's something no photograph, no memory, can re-create. And Sam didn't respond, just breathed in the air's bite and tang and felt the cold caress the back of his neck, his face and hands; and shortly after she rolled the window up she directed him inland again, through farmlands bordered by farrowed fields or overgrown pastures and finally through areas not as thinly populated, the rural outskirts of what he imagined must be a nearby town. The narrow roads became streets, and he slowed to stay within the speed limit, then slowed again when she warned him that they'd be pulling in to a driveway to the right, not a hundred feet on.

When he parked, Claire didn't move right away, just stayed where she was and took in the bunker-like, two-story structure that had no windows, the high, solid wall that joined it. This, she said after a moment, is where Iris—my mother—lives. I'm not going to introduce you, but I'd appreciate it if you'd come with me as far as her patio. I'll be only a few minutes.

The book, he said, as she got out of the car with that camera slung over her shoulder.

It's not for her.

The door that led through the wall wasn't locked, and he followed Claire through it. He hadn't expected paradise, but this world unto itself—perfectly enclosed—presented a Babylonian autumn of manicured trees and bushes and grasses and flowers and herbs through which wound paved pathways that ended, at the far end of the garden, in a long leanto and what seemed to be a shed, while to one side of the main house with its patio and wisteria'd pergola and French doors, halfway down the garden's length, stood a cottage with its own porch. The size of the spread, the loveliness of the house and cottage and garden, so engrossed him that, looking elsewhere and everywhere, he bumped into Claire when she stopped in her tracks at the sight of a child whom Sam heard before he saw, the boy calling out *Are you here to see Grandma?* and coming toward them at a run. Sorry, Sam murmured to Claire, who turned to him with a puzzled look on her face that gave way to a frown because a girl—how young or how old, Sam couldn't tell—suddenly rose from a crouch at the far end of the garden and began to raise a hand in greeting, then dropped it as Claire turned her back on her and the child, on Sam, and determinedly strode onto the patio of the main house and let herself in.

The boy stopped where he was then, a short distance from Sam. He toed something on the path, looked up at Sam, asked again: Are you here to see Grandma?

Nope, Sam said.

Why not?

I don't really know her.

Oh, the child replied with a shrug, again toeing the path, first with one foot, then the other, before asking Do you want to see some rosehips? as the girl at the garden's end called out *Luke!* twice, the child turning around and looking in her direction and then back at Sam. They're *really* big, the boy said. Okay, Sam replied, and the boy moved off and Sam followed to where rosebushes heavy with hips were pointed out, Luke then telling Sam that his turtle had dug a home beneath the rock ledge behind the bushes. You can't see him now, he said solemnly, because turtles sleep for a long time when it's cold.

Does he have a name? Sam asked.

Yes, and he knows it. But even if we call him, he won't hear us now. He can't wake up until spring.

Well, he'll be pretty rested by then.

Yes, the boy agreed, looking at Sam very seriously. How come your face is funny?

Luke, the girl said gently in admonishment, her voice startling Sam, for she was very close, had come upon them quietly. I'm *so* sorry —

It's okay, Sam interrupted her, feeling the color rise to his face, seeing her blush as well. He's not even four yet, she apologized, looking squarely at Sam, Sam having the queer feeling that she hadn't noticed or wouldn't ever notice his deformity; she wasn't staring but just gazing at him shyly, and there was a quiet shyness to the way she held herself, placed her hands on Luke's shoulders. She didn't seem to him old enough to be the mother of this or any child. She was willowy in the way of some girls on the cusp of adolescence, gracefully gangly, long-limbed and loose-wristed; and her plain face was so flawless, the color of her eyes so remarkable because so pale, so indistinct, her expression despite that blush so serene, she seemed ageless, like those classic depictions of angels. My name's Luke, the boy said, as though to clarify any misunderstanding, and Sam solemnly reached out and shook the child's hand and replied, I'm Sam. June, was all she said by way of introduction, but she extended her hand and Sam took it and something passed between them, or into him, and he felt himself so unsettled that he forgot to let go, and for an odd moment he, they, stood there like former lovers who were amazed to have found each other again. And then she broke the spell, her blush deepening, cupped Luke's chin and looked down at him and said, C'mon now, I need help breaking up the squash vines before it gets dark, and the boy immediately spread his arms like wings and pretended to fly as he ran off down the path toward the back of the garden. Great kid, Sam said, but she was looking beyond him, and he turned to see Claire closing the door behind her and on the patio pausing, holding up a set of keys, indicating with a nod of her head the outside door and again ignoring June's tentative wave. Sam said, Maybe next time, as June dropped her hand. He heard her soft *Bye* behind his back, caught up with Claire—who locked the outside door behind them—and got behind the wheel. He didn't know whether there'd be a next time or why he'd said that to June, or why he wanted Claire to acknowledge the girl, the child; he never spoke impulsively and yet he had; he wasn't one to fantasize and yet he might have imagined the current he'd thought, felt, had passed from her to him, back.

Claire's expression was frozen, inscrutable, her body stiff with tension, her voice falsely modulated as she gave directions. He did not ask who the girl in the garden was, or the child who'd called Claire's mother *Grandma*; if Claire even knew, she didn't appear willing to acknowledge the existence of either, and that kept him from inquiring. They were on the road for less than half an hour, and before he'd cut the engine at the end of a long dirt drive that led to a farmhouse, Claire was out of the car and running toward the man who had stepped from the house and off the porch with open arms, catching her in an embrace that rocked them together solemnly until he pulled back to look at her, took her face in his hands, kissed her forehead as though in benediction, and then locked his arms around her again. They paid no mind to the dogs—both large, of indeterminable breed—that came from around back of the house and slipped through the split-rail fencing and circled the two joyfully, their harmless barking probably instigating the appearance of a pinto pony and dun-colored horse that appeared from whence the dogs had come and, aroused by canine ruckus, trotted to the fence where they stopped short and bobbed their heads—as if in agreement, or approval—over the topmost rail.

Sam waited where he was and exchanged the sunglasses for his eyepatch. The afternoon was already gone; if he were to drive much farther and at night, he'd have to do so with the patch up or take his chances without depth perception. He had no idea this was the end of the line until Claire and Oldman approached, Oldman quieting and shooing the dogs, his arm around Claire's shoulders and hers about his waist until they reached the car and Oldman opened the door like a butler, Claire continuing to cling to him, saying, Oldman, Sam, Sam, Oldman. A handshake with Sam still behind the wheel, Oldman smiling broadly and telling him, C'mon, let's get you both settled. And Sam took a moment to recover, both from the unwelcome realization that Claire had arranged for him, them, to stay in someone's home, and from the shock of seeing that discolored scar that could in no way be ameliorated or hidden, streaking a lightning zigzag across Oldman's face. Oldman had Sam's duffel and Claire's camera bag in hand before Sam got to his feet, and Claire, carrying a small suitcase, asked Sam in a whisper to reach in and retrieve the book. She didn't look over her shoulder at the sound of him closing, almost slamming, the driver's door.

Sam was settled onto a floor of his own, in a long, narrow alcove with two single beds that hugged the straight wall, a bureau between them; opposite the bureau a screened window sat within the steep slope of a beam-striated ceiling. He left his duffel unpacked, went back through the open landing whose walls were lined with bookcases, before which sat two armchairs--horsehide, Oldman had told him--each with a reading lamp. Across the landing, he entered what had been a master bedroom but was now what Oldman termed a museum; the walls were hung with old farm implements, bridle bits and horseshoes wrought for humongous creatures, wooden yokes, cowbells, tintype photographs; the furnishings included an adze-carved rocking cradle, a captain's bed—its curved headrest and sculpted feet, and most likely its frame, of wrought iron, its mattress ticking stuffed with straw, its cover a hand-stitched quilt—and a rough-hewn rocking chair, one pedal-operated Singer sewing machine, a large oval-shaped rag rug, crocheted and knitted throws. The bathroom located off the museum room was, Sam realized, four times the size of the one in his—no, his brother's—apartment: aside from the toilet, there was a tin bathtub, rigged for a shower as well as soaking;

a porcelain sink set into what had once been a stand for a large washbasin; rough-planked shelves that held hatboxes, soaps, towels, stoneware water pitchers; free-standing towel racks.

He walked back to the alcove room, stood before the window. Leaves resembling whorling flocks of small misshapen birds spiraled sideways through the dusk's graphite solidity, catching silently and stationary on the dark pasture grounds. Before long, night would press into being. Oldman had told Sam to come down—Claire echoing—whenever he wanted. But Sam didn't want to socialize, couldn't; he stood disoriented and ill at ease, tired; the driving, the memories, the halting, Claire's silence, the driving on, this arrival: he hadn't contemplated being settled in a home, he hadn't come to know the woman he accompanied and had no idea who Oldman was. It's his fault, he told himself, for convincing himself he could do Leonard this favor, and he couldn't blame Claire for assuming—despite how alike he and Claire might be, each determined to remain unknowable, unassailable—that he'd be comfortable with a floor to himself, left to himself, left *here*. His fault, his fault: he didn't know Claire well enough at all, hadn't thought things through, and was now wrangling with how to admit that being here, in a stranger's home, had flooded him with that deep sense of alienation he'd suffered when he first returned home from the hospital and realized himself stupefied, insensate, and for the longest time incapable of desiring anything other than nothingness.

A motel room would have suited; he could have managed a drink or two at a bar among strangers, and he wouldn't have minded driving on up the coast. He now wanted nothing more than to leave, go elsewhere and anywhere of his choosing, journey on with or without her—without, it would have to be: Claire had reached her destination and would stay as long as she needed or wanted. He could hear the drift of indistinguishable words from downstairs, but he couldn't bring himself to confront her now, instead decided he'd survive this one evening and tell her in the morning of his intention to leave, maybe stay on his own elsewhere nearby and explore the coast should she relinquish the car to him, and if not, return to the city. The decision steadies him for a second, then upsets him—for if she asks why, he won't be able to explain, he can't express reasons that are beyond his comprehension. Surely she'd ask why: she'd reached her destination, he'd seen her embraced by Oldman, saw that benedictory kiss that altered Sam's vision of what he'd considered to be Claire's inflexibly cold reserve, her unyielding physicality, watched Claire soften, meld into Oldman, become malleable, show herself to be delighted when Oldman held her intense, perfect face in his hands. Who she is, Sam couldn't guess, but he knew she would indeed ask why he'd want to leave Oldman's. A shrug, he considered, would not suffice to signal his distress at being a stranger among strangers.

He moved from the window, removed his shoes, stretched out on the bed, let the cadence of their voices wash over him as he wished himself gone. He later awoke in a fetal position, facing the wall, to the sound of the car pulling away. It took a moment to orient himself, remember where he was. The house was mute. He eventually swung his legs over the side of the bed and rose, and in stocking feet took the stairs. The landing and stairwell night-lights were on, as was a corner lamp in the livingroom and an overhead in the passage to the kitchen. He walked through both and was in the room before he realized that Oldman—who'd looked up from the cookbook Claire had given him—was at the table.

Sorry, I didn't think anyone was—

I was just about to fetch a beer, Oldman said, and now I'll fetch two. Have a seat.

Oldman wasn't a man to be refused, there was an assurance to his voice, a firm kindliness, and he gestured as he got up that Sam was to sit anywhere he pleased. He went into the pantry and returned to find Sam still standing. Claire tells me you're a cook, Oldman said, so I hope you don't mind sitting around the kitchen. I've worked to keep the place pretty much as it was, and although my father took the liberty of replacing the hand pump—which I remember—with faucets a long time ago, I've had no reason to get rid of the tin sink, or close up the fireplace, or replace this old cooker-stove, or do anything but mop down the flagstone floor. Anyway—he handed Sam an opened beer and a glass, pulled a chair out for him—we always used it as a family room, the livingroom was only for special occasions until TV came along, and I still spend most of my time in here, pretending to think if I'm not cooking, sometimes pretending to think while cooking. Please, sit down, Sam—and Sam finally did as Oldman set his own beer and glass down, then brought out shot glasses and a bottle of whisky, which he placed in the center of the table. For chasers, Oldman said. And then was gone again, reappearing with a ramekin of cold chicken in aspic and a side of small, perfectly round potatoes in a sauce Sam couldn't identify.

The beer, which Sam followed with a shot of whisky, was followed by another, then a second whisky. Oldman prompted Sam to try the chicken, told him the aspic was nothing more than chicken broth gelled. Told him, too, how he came to discover cooking during the war, that he'd sometimes billeted with families—what was left of them—who seemed able to make a dinner from nothing, an omelet from an onion and one egg, soup from a few carrots or turnips and a bone, wild greens tenderized by cooking slowly with a piece of fatback or bacon or any fowl fat; that was in France, but Germany was another matter, even in the countryside there was hardly anything to be found, everything had been pilfered or consumed or destroyed by the war's end; everyone needed to be fed, everyone was scrounging, foraging, what with the defeat and the enormous confusion caused by displaced populations and the massive destruction resulting from the Allied air raids; at any rate, the country was basically stripped of anything edible but what people had hidden, had somehow preserved, which is why, Oldman said, he developed a taste for mustard and pickles and K rations there. He went on, telling Sam — who was surprised by the texture and taste of the chicken and potatoes set before him, and who quietly finished both along with a third beer, another whisky — that he'd never been at the front, that as a photographer assigned to the mop-up troops who followed Patton's push through France and into Germany he'd never seen action, for which he was grateful, as it had been hard enough witnessing what he'd chronicled. And Sam felt the warmth from the whisky work its magic, he relaxed back, drank more, listened, occasionally lost the thread of Oldman's one-sided conversation as he absently wondered who Oldman was to Claire, how old he might be — fifty or seventy, Sam couldn't tell, the man was slender, his movements fluid, he had a full head of salt-and-pepper hair but there was no telling what that meant — as Oldman went thoughtfully on, recounting to Sam how he'd found solace in simple food and those families with whom he sometimes billeted, and in the camaraderie he found among the troops. There's a lot to be said, Oldman told him, for a democratic army in which everyone who can, serves. That war pulled together boys and men from all forty-eight states and from all walks of life who, despite their differences, had to find and indeed found common ground in the fight against fascism — though that had been lost in Spain, Oldman noted — and thank the powers that be for the Russians because, no matter what you think of them, without them all of Europe might have been *sieg heil*-ing for decades. Sam waved off another beer and instead helped himself to the whisky again, sat satiated and more than mildly inebriated and somewhat stunned by how comfortable he'd begun to feel in Oldman's presence, how soothing it was to listen to Oldman's melodic voice, to someone who, in another time and place, might have been the keeper of tribal history, the chronicler of all that had come before, the bard who sang of what was past and would come to be. The damndest thing is, Oldman continued after a longish pause, in those years I served I was never sick, never had so much as a sniffle, never suffered more than a few cuts and bruises, never got hurt. He traced the scar on his face and told Sam: Actually, the *damndest* thing is, I got this from a monkey.

Sam didn't know if he'd heard correctly. He cocked his head slightly and the movement induced vertigo, the room swam behind Oldman, and Sam leaned back and steadied himself — his joints were liquid, he was losing his balance — as Oldman said laughingly, That's right, a monkey. Sam began laughing too, the room was no longer reeling but somehow expanding, contracting, as Oldman went on to ask: So, what happened to you? — and then Sam's chest was heaving, a strangled sound came from him as he began sobbing into his hands, his tears salty and the taste of them bitter and Sam unabashed and anguished. For no one — not his parents or his brother, not Freddie, neither Rita nor Gloria, not Leonard, no one — had ever asked; they'd seen him, they'd seen what had become of him,

Rita had often touched his scars, and maybe they'd all waited for Sam to recount what he'd been through, but their silence only reinforced his impression that they all, every last one of them, willed his story to remain untold, his past unspoken. *Oh god,* he finally managed, the words guttural through his ragged breathing, *oh god,* and then he wiped at his face with his hands and saw Oldman through a blur, and in a voice he doesn't even recognize begins to haltingly tell what he has never told anyone, haltingly because he is drunk and because he has never put what happened that day into words, he's lived with the impression of it for six years, been reminded of it every time he's seen his reflection or seen in the reflection of others' eyes the pity, disgust, shock — for his face is shocking, even with that eyepatch — and he hears himself begin to describe that day, knows he is telling a disjointed tale. He'd had a bad feeling, guys got those, everyone at one time or other gave in to their premonitions, he was seventeen days away from discharge and they'd been sniped at that morning and maybe were in pursuit of they knew not how many Vietcong and by late afternoon had seen nothing, not been engaged again, the Cong had a way of disappearing into the ground, or the paddies, or the air, the country was a mass of tunnels, there were interminable swamps, endless jungles. The heat was hellish, unbearable, the mission unclear, and Sam had had this awful feeling, his sweat tasted sour from his conviction, his fear, that his number was up, and then they'd stepped out from the forest into a small clearing and saw the hamlet encircled by paddies and also saw what might have been an old man or woman — who could tell, everyone wore the same loose black pajama-like shirts and pants, everyone looked alike at a distance — sitting, no, leaning against a dike, the bottom half of the figure submerged in the paddy, not moving, not bothering to get up and run, just motionless under a conical hat; and as they drew nearer a wind kicked up and the hat and head suddenly tilted back and Sam was looking at—and being stared at by—the dead, the cadaver's face bereft of nose and eyes and lips, strands of blackened skin clinging in skeins to its skull, the sight was horrible and to Sam ominous. They torched the empty hamlet, went back the same way they'd come, kept to the narrow trail in silence. Sam was unable to shake off that skull's gaze and eventually his knees gave way, he became sick to his stomach and stopped to vomit, heaving as quietly as he could, the men behind him halting—he'd been on point—and waiting for him to go on, but he couldn't get to his feet, not just then, so the others passed him as two men helped to raise him, steady him, before pushing him forward. A minute later, or moments later, all hell broke loose. The trip wire—*It was meant for me,* Sam said, almost choking on his words, his breathing still ragged—entangled one of the men who'd passed Sam by, and three men paid for that with their lives. The soldier in front of Sam was blown to the side and landed on another mine—*That was meant for me too,* Sam said brokenly—and didn't survive.

He hadn't looked at Oldman, now reached for the whisky, took a deep breath and poured, downed, another shot: he had nothing else to say except that he couldn't remember anything more, he'd regained consciousness without sight, his head was bandaged around his eyes, he was in pain. He shook his head in anguish, met Oldman's eyes. Son, Oldman told him, those mines didn't have anyone's name on them. Not yours, not theirs.

Oldman then pushed his chair back, rose, and put a hand on Sam's shoulder before clearing the table, rinsing the dishes in the sink. Sam sat dumbly, like a man stunned, fingering the empty shot glass, focusing on the whisky bottle, trying to keep himself from falling over, the room from spinning, feeling that kindly word *son* flow through him, course in his veins: not even his father had called him that, no officer or nurse or doctor — not even Freddie — had ever put a consoling hand on his shoulder, and now Oldman, whom Sam didn't know and to whom he'd told what he'd always imagined would kill him with the telling, returned to the table and put his hand on Sam's shoulder again. You'll want to turn in, Oldman said, and Sam nodded, let Oldman help him stand — he was drained, drunk — and keep him upright as he staggered slowly through the hallway, over the livingroom's pitching floor, up the swirling stairs, Oldman pulling one of Sam's arms over his shoulder, holding it by the wrist, encircling Sam's waist with his free arm, supporting him, guiding him carefully through the house and finally into his, Sam's, room. He let Sam down gently onto the bed and removed his shoes, left, then returned with an afghan and covered him.

Sorry, Sam managed to mumble.

Don't be, came Oldman's response.

June

IRIS SAID, That was my daughter who came yesterday.
She didn't mention Claire's name, and although June
waited for her to continue Iris turned her attention to Luke
in her lap, took up the book he was holding and opened it, began to read to him. June busied herself with the late-morning
routine she'd settled into and which she and Iris had never discussed, just as they'd never conferred as to how much Iris's needs
had changed. For in the beginning of June's tenure—which Mabel and June and Iris had assumed temporary—Iris evidenced
no desire for help, for June's presence; she'd had a tremor in one
arm and sometimes dragged one of her legs behind her but pretended to be otherwise hale, and the only request she'd made
was that June bring Luke to her every morning at a certain
hour, for a certain length of time.

It was through Luke that they came to be as familiar with
each other as any relationship centered on a child allows, espe-

cially as June was, for a long while, intimidated by Iris's impenetrable remoteness, for Iris did nothing to alter the way she lived, the way she was, and never once asked June about herself. But they slowly became used to each other during that first fall and winter, as Iris accustomed herself to the girl's comings and goings—June was prompt each morning, not a moment late, and on time to pick Luke up after Iris requested she be left alone with him—and Iris eventually began to talk to June about the baby. Iris knew a great deal about infants and, without mentioning that she'd ever had a child of her own, began to smooth June's way through single motherhood and moderate the girl's ignorance, assuage her fears; Iris knew how to relieve teething pain, whether a rash or runny nose was serious, when June should expect the baby to become steady on his feet, to talk. Iris never broached the subject of June's—and Luke's—transition back to Mabel's until one morning after that first winter, when she announced almost savagely: I've decided to tell Mabel you'll be staying here.

June was startled. The uncertainty in her gaze, her voiceless reaction, took Iris aback. I'll eventually need help permanently, Iris told her gruffly, and Mabel will understand that. So if you want—

I'd like for us to stay, June said.

Then it's settled.

But I'd like to be useful.

That will come, Iris asserted. And although Iris asked nothing more of her than to continue bringing Luke over in the mornings, she now acknowledged June's presence less grudgingly, and by late spring they were working shoulder to shoulder in the garden, sometimes lunching and more and more often sitting quietly together during early evenings in Iris's house with Luke amusing them. The isolation June had suffered during that first fall and winter had almost undone her; she'd never felt so completely alone, facing nothing but a void during those first months at Iris's, each week passing exactly like the other and June barely able to contend with a lonesomeness that—like the boundless ocean she'd once walked into, the endless country she'd left behind—simply stretched limitless before her. There was Luke to care for, the cottage to keep up, the cursory Friday meetings with Duncan—Duncan always cordial but lawyer-like, unwilling to discuss the fact that Iris didn't say much more than hello and goodbye to June when she brought Luke to and retrieved him from Iris each morning, just judiciously telling June in that noncommittal even voice that if Iris chose to break the ice then it would be broken and if she didn't so choose then June was not to worry herself, was there anyone June wanted to telephone? And she always shook her head, let herself and Luke be ushered out by Oldman, who drove her to and from Duncan's, sometimes persuaded her to let him take her shopping, and always took her and Luke to the Puritan.

Oldman was her lifeline that first autumn, familiarizing her with streets and lanes and alleys, shops and the library, citing the town's history and oddities, telling how the factories and mills had once worked nonstop and how they'd come to close, what the now quiet port had been like when commerce was thriving, how the cobblestones that yet lined the factory yards and streets and canal walkways had crossed the ocean in ships as ballast. He spoke to her as though he could make June a part of what she wasn't, not then—in actuality, not even now—perhaps believing that certain things were settled forever, that June was settled forever, would never leave. His kindly and, to June, inexplicable interest in her, not to mention the situation in which she found herself, added to a perplexity that ate away at and at times consumed her. Oldman, she eventually confided to him, I don't know why I'm here, I mean, Iris has no use for me. And he'd studied the fried clams on his plate before telling her: Life's a bit of a riddle, June. In my experience, things either work out or they don't, but fretting isn't going to solve anything.

Her time with Oldman initially seemed dreamlike, especially because Friday evenings—after she and Luke were dropped off—were the harshest, almost impossible to face as autumn gave way to winter. The darkness June closed the door against settled in earlier each afternoon and lasted later each morning, and within that darkness she was isolate, trapped. She wondered whether Oldman had sensed this or just knew what it was to endure loneliness, to be so adrift. Not that she wasn't thankful to have a place of her own, she was, far removed from the trailers she'd lived in all her life, let alone Ward's annex in that houseful of men; and she had Luke, and they were safe and warm and wanted for nothing; but she was at odds and lost despite having Luke to love and despite whiling away the long evenings knitting, sewing by hand, eventually sitting motionless, curling within herself, and listening to her son's breathing. Sleep often refused to overtake her because she was unable to understand for the life of her why she had a roof over her head, why either of the two women to whom she was utterly beholden had given her and Luke shelter, had indeed given her everything but a future. The contemplation of its emptiness left June disoriented, for she didn't know how she would make her own way, stand firm, if tomorrow or during the following week or month she'd have to.

But Iris came to need June's help, perhaps as much as Iris needed Luke to love, and June eventually came to feel settled, secure. Now, behind her back, Iris and Luke began to laugh, the child wanton with joy, and June smiled to herself, mashed the boiled potatoes with milk and butter, then cut up one of the pork chops she'd fried—Iris was no longer able to handle a knife and fork in tandem—and hesitated before cutting the other, asking over her shoulder: Will your daughter come to lunch? Or should I make something else for dinner?

No and no, Iris replied in a cartoon character voice, as if her answer were part of the story she was reading to Luke. The mashed potatoes and pork chops would last, then, through tomorrow: Iris hadn't had an appetite in months, ate little and erratically. June—whom Oldman had told of Claire's impending arrival—wondered how shocked Claire must have been upon seeing her mother. No matter that seventeen years had passed since they'd last laid eyes on each other, what ailed Iris had little to do with aging. Iris refused to name the illness or discuss it—she'd finally seen doctors over the last year, Duncan arranging the appointments and secreting her off to offices and hospitals for consultations, tests and diagnoses Iris never mentioned—and was tight-lipped about her progressive debilitation and the prescribed drugs she was given. Her tremors were now pronounced, the fingers of one hand had curled uselessly inward, and she'd suffered muscle and weight loss so extreme that her bones appeared to erupt through her papery skin. She relied on canes, more often on a walker, not only because she was weak and given to spasms but also because there was no telling when she'd lose what little balance she had; and despite this, Iris insisted on rising alone and washing herself, dressing herself, putting herself to bed, on being on her feet and about although she could no longer cook for herself. Toward late summer she'd finally succumbed to sitting rather than working alongside June in the garden—harvesting the vegetables and fruit, weeding, pruning, composting and turning over the soil—which had moved June to a pity she didn't dare reveal.

Lunch, June announced when Iris and Luke had finished with the book, but Iris shook her head, told her, I'll eat later. Me too, Luke said, and June retrieved him from Iris's lap, carried him toward the door and quelled his protest by observing that Iris was tired and now needed to nap. Iris waved goodbye with her good hand, blew the child a kiss, and then June stepped into the dead chill with Luke in her arms, let him squirm free on Iris's patio, watched him race into the garden to check for any sign of the turtle. She took a deep breath, savored the air's frigid sting: she has come to love this time of year, when autumn lies on the cusp of winter, shoulders into the next season, and the garden is fallow, the fruit trees without fruit, the rosebushes bursting with fat shiny hips, the maple and birch and ash and oak almost stripped of leaves that had flamed yellow, orange, red, or rusted to sepia before fading and dropping. The frost was already powdering the garden at night, and although winter might continue to lurk around the corner, there was no telling; that first fall at Iris's the snow had come before the deciduous trees were completely denuded—there had been a prolonged Indian summer—and June had been shocked at how winter had simply erupted without warning, the snow falling straight and heavy and silent, unlike how it fell sideways—blown on wailing winds—where she was from.

There hadn't been a whisper of a breeze, and June had woken to a snow-blanketed world of silence and windows laced with crystalline freeze. The garden was beautiful—its bushes bowed beneath weighty clumps of shimmer, the underside branches of its trees wetly dark, the leaves on those branches wearing coats of crinkled powder — under that layer of alabaster. She'd broken through the foot-deep snow with Luke in her arms and delivered him to Iris exactly on time, then taken a shovel from the shed and cleared a path to the cottage porch, then to Iris's, and swept the snow off the patio edges before shoveling a lane to the outside door and clearing the driveway to the mailbox and street. She had warmed to the rhythm of the work, enjoyed the heft of the snow, marveled at the glowering unbroken cloudcover. For the first time at Iris's, she felt as though she were earning her keep. And, for the first time, Iris said more than hello and goodbye to her, telling June in a conversational tone that the first snow often heralded Thanksgiving, which happened to be the next day.

I take it, Iris had gone on, that Duncan's made arrangements for tomorrow that include you.

Oldman Smith invited us to dinner in the afternoon.

I expect you'll still bring Luke in the morning.

Yes, of course.

Good, Iris had responded. She disentangled a strand of her hair from Luke's grasp, held him high and jostled him in midair, making him laugh, then gave him to June. Tomorrow then, she affirmed. And as June opened the door, added: You might want to stack some cordwood on your porch rather than running out for an armful every time you feel like using the fireplace.

I didn't know it was okay to use the wood. Or make a fire.

Go right ahead. I no longer do.

And while Iris had Luke the next morning, June swept the paths she'd shoveled the day before and stacked cordwood on the cottage porch, then retrieved her son and dressed them both for Oldman's. Duncan arrived in Oldman's Studebaker as she was locking the outside door behind her, and he got out and opened and closed the rear door for her and Luke, introduced her to Meredith, who was in the front seat—and who, Duncan said, teaches high school. Luke was quiet, watchful, as they drove the plowed road that gleamed darkly between the snowbanks edging white-strewn fields and pastures and tinseled forests and snowcapped roofs atop homes and farms that reminded June of Christmas card scenes. She too was quiet, watchful, as always somewhat awkward with Duncan, now shy because of Meredith, and apprehensive because she didn't know what to expect; she'd never been to Oldman's and had never celebrated Thanksgiving, hadn't ever even heard of Thanksgiving before going to school, where she and the other children were taught to draw blackclad Pilgrims in buckled shoes and strange hats, enormous brown turkeys with fanned tails and red crests, and were introduced to the holiday's mythology and the feast to be reenacted, which her mother, whether at the trailer or not, ignored. We didn't come from Pilgrims, what crap, her mother spat out upon glancing at the only Pilgrim-turkey-wilderness drawing June ever took home. What lazy bastards teachers are, her mother continued in a fury, instead of teaching they sit around with their feet up while you kids draw stupid stuff.

Auntie, to whom June had later given the drawing and who had taped it over one of the windows already covered with newspaper, told her: Problem with your mother is that she ain't ever thought she's got anything to be thankful about, except maybe her own two feet. Now, my people were grateful to feast whenever they could, but they never did take to the notion of setting aside one day a year to celebrate their thanks, especially as there was no telling whether there'd be anything on the table. You can't count on good times just because you're supposed to, and there's no pretending otherwise.

And the pristine scenery flowed slowly by, Duncan behind the wheel, June wondering if her mother still lived in that trailer heavy with cigarette smoke, the rug stained with beer and coffee and liquor spills, the smell of burning dust given off by the electric heater; and if she was still alive, whether at this moment she was walking off, wordlessly passing by Auntie and maybe those two men who came and went in that high-cabbed truck, her mother not looking at them standing near the drive, refusing to see them and heedless of the wind that buffeted her gait and made the electric wires sing and the trailers shudder and creak and list, her mother heedless and just heading off as she always did, following a spiraled circle that led from the outside in, the one—Auntie always said—June's mother had been marked from birth to walk. Which was, according to Auntie, not June's path.

And it won't ever be yours, June promised Luke silently as they pulled into Oldman's, the sight of which astonished June. The farmhouse seemed to her immense, picture-postcard perfect; but she found herself even more astounded by one of Oldman's dogs that materialized to greet them, for it was so similar to the dog which had harried and rescued her and Luke at the shore—it had that creature's coloring and shagginess and size, the same gold-specked dark eyes, and it circled her and Luke in the drive with the same bounding joy she'd never forget—that she later couldn't quite bring herself to believe Oldman when he told her he'd had the dog for many years and that it had never left the property. Or later bring herself to quite believe that for the rest of that day, at Oldman's with Duncan and Meredith and Luke, she hadn't been under a spell.

They'd feasted, and she never told them that this was her first Thanksgiving meal, that she was overwhelmed by Oldman's table, with its fish and fowl—he explained to her that he tried to be as true to the first Thanksgiving as possible—and corn pudding, squashes, potatoes, mushrooms, baked apples. They made her feel welcome, Oldman and Meredith—and even Duncan, as much as he trusted himself to—fussing over Luke, no one asking anything of June, no one mentioning Iris, and she sat and ate and listened to the others talk over the course of the afternoon about local people and affairs June knew nothing about. She wasn't uncomfortable at all, but wasn't drawn into the conversation until late in the day, when Meredith—who had a passion for handmade quilts and had knocked on the doors of families who had what she described as one-of-a-kind heirlooms, which she wanted to document before they disintegrated or disappeared—was told by Oldman that June had been taught to sew by hand as a child and did so yet. Meredith didn't hesitate, she immediately asked June if she'd be interested in examining the quilts she'd found, explain to Meredith the various stitches, perhaps even duplicate them? Oldman, she said, had already offered to photograph the quilts, create an archive of what he called Meredith's rescue-from-oblivion project. When June hesitated, Meredith—thinking her reluctance might be due to having no one to watch Luke—told her of course she expected June to bring the baby along, no one would mind; but it was Duncan who, with a meaningful look, said he'd make sure Oldman and Meredith respected what he called, in his lawyerly fashion, June's legitimate obligations. At which Meredith had told June:

You know, we could arrange to do it on Sunday afternoons, it's easiest to see people then—

And afterward have dinner here, Oldman interjected, at which June caught Duncan's surprised expression; he'd raised his eyebrows and sat back, ruminating as if disturbed. June didn't know that Duncan had only recently broken his long-standing tradition of spending Sunday afternoons alone with Oldman, for he'd brought Meredith into the mix, and was simply reacting to the notion that those Sunday afternoons would now include June and Luke as well. Not that Duncan would have said he objected to Meredith's suggestion, but Oldman's swift reaction, his obvious attachment to the girl and her child, left Duncan to again consider that Oldman appeared to be repeating history by taking to this girl who now lived at Iris's, in what had been Claire's cottage; indeed, Duncan was so wary of Oldman's eagerness to include June, nestle her ever more firmly under his wing, that he later, when alone with Oldman, said emphatically—not to admonish but to clearly state—*Oldman, she's not Claire.* To which Oldman as emphatically replied, *That's what I'm counting on,* despite sensing that his rejoinder might have cut to the quick, suspecting that Duncan—who had never admitted to Oldman or anyone else that he hadn't allowed himself to utter the words that would have stayed Claire, kept her close—had, for many years and perhaps even now, felt Claire's absence as his loss.

June—because of Duncan's expression, the backward shift in his chair—hesitated, but Meredith continued on, telling June how she'd come to be interested in such an arcane craft no longer practiced by hand and almost dead now—hardly anyone made quilts anymore—pausing only when Oldman left to answer the phone and then going silent when he returned and said to Dun-

can, Claire's on the line. Duncan didn't excuse himself, just per-
emptorily placed a hand on Meredith's shoulder as he rose, then
wordlessly left the room. Meredith looked suddenly abashed,
somewhat lost, and it took her a moment to recover, manage a
smile, return to persuading June to join her, them, on those future Sundays. June didn't yet know who Claire was, and she
didn't ask, instead watchfully listened to Meredith again until
Meredith interrupted herself when Duncan returned to the table and remarked to Oldman, So she's quit the newspaper — you
never said.

Well, after all, Oldman stated evenly, she's always had a way
of letting you know in her own time.

Duncan didn't respond, and Meredith looked to hold her
breath. I'm going to show June the rest of the house, Oldman
said, and he took June and Luke through the rooms on each of
the three floors. He didn't hurry, took his time reminiscing as
to what the house had been like when three generations lived
in it, which rooms had been inhabited by his parents and pa-
ternal grandparents, how the place had been added on to, what
he'd done to repair and restore the flooring and wainscoting in
places; how, despite having electricity since he could remember, they'd had iceboxes rather than a refrigerator and a wood-
stove in which — the summer heat be damned — his mother
and grandmother baked bread twice a week; that they had indoor plumbing and running water in the upstairs bathrooms
but a hand pump, long since replaced, in the kitchen; that the
curtains had been sewn by his mother and her mother, the rag
rug hooked by hand, the farm implements now hanging on the
walls mostly forged by blacksmiths. June was silent, seemingly
intimidated, until they came to examine the quilt in what he
called the museum room, at which she came to life as he encour-

aged her to indeed agree to be a part of Meredith's—and now his—plan.

Which she did. It took time for June to grow used to being part of a small circle, to understand that she was useful to Meredith—she was adept at copying the quilting stitches and patterns—and that Oldman, whose reasons for looking out for her she never questioned nor quite understood, delighted in her company, that even Duncan slowly gave over to being less officious with her. And that Iris, removed from that circle, had eventually opened herself—not her arms, only Luke was allowed her embraces—in the only way she could to June, which was through her evolving needs and ongoing illness and her dogged absorption in raising and loving Luke.

Three years on, and none of them—Oldman, Duncan, Meredith, Iris—had ever asked June about her past or about her future, which she only considered in terms of continuing what she was doing and in terms of what she would feel when Luke began school. Oldman eventually saw to it that June opened a savings account and became an indispensable member of his Sunday clique, and he watched her admiration for the craftsmanship he and Meredith documented evolve into a confidence in her own talents, for she was now quilting, creating her own patterns, and making bedcovers for Oldman and Meredith, Iris and Mabel, Luke; and she hadn't forgotten her abandonment, but the anguish with which she'd been crushed had lessened, she'd learned to trust the present, which allowed her fear of the future to diminish, so that now—June looking out over the garden, sitting on the porch stoop and watching the squirrels busy themselves, calculating that their heavy coats presaged an early, hard winter—with Claire present because Iris had called and told her *It's time, I need to see you,* and without June knowing the reason but suspecting, sensing, the change to come, June continued to draw on an inner strength born of the stability she'd been granted here by chance.

And Iris was right: Claire didn't appear for lunch or dinner or at all, not that day or the next. Iris didn't mention her daughter further, and June didn't ask. She wouldn't have known that Claire had finally returned to see her mother had Sam not knocked on the cottage door to tell June that Claire had asked him to let her know they were here, that she might be a while with Iris, that she wanted to speak to June, that she'd be by later. Hands in pockets, Sam hunched in the chill—he was wearing a woolen hunting shirt June recognized as Oldman's over a light sweater—and stood just beyond the door June hadn't fully opened. She caught the scent of woodsmoke from her fireplace's chimney and saw it wisp by in blue strands above and beyond Sam, who looked away as if in embarrassment, then cleared his throat to ask if he might come in, wait for Claire, and for a few seconds she stood dumbstruck until Sam awkwardly added: If it's no bother—I mean, she might be a while. Of course, how rude of me, come in, June apologized, and closed the door behind her first visitor; Oldman has never set foot in the cottage, this haven has remained inviolable out of June's respect for Iris's privacy and also because she's never considered having company here, not even Meredith. And now, she thinks, this: this tall, lean man, a perfect stranger, whom Luke is delighted to see and who seems even more uncomfortable and shy than June but who pulls up a chair and sits at the table with the boy, talks with him as Luke finishes putting the final pieces of a puzzle in place while June adds a few pieces of cordwood to the fire and then sits before it. And within a half-hour—they haven't spoken, he's been involved with her son—Sam takes a seat in the other armchair that faces the blaze, Luke settling into his lap: and she is, as always, amazed at how loving Luke is, how trusting, having long enjoyed both Iris's and Oldman's arms and attentions, as he now leans back against Sam's chest, the two of them silently gazing at the flames. Sam doesn't turn to her — the damaged side of his face and that eyepatch are to the wall, the profile she sees is unblemished, even handsome, the man has high cheekbones and an aquiline nose, full mouth, chiseled jaw — when he speaks, just stays as he is and says, It's been a long time since I've held a kid. How long? Luke asks, and Sam takes a deep breath, breathes out. About six years, he answers. He doesn't explain — but he later told Oldman — that the last child he had in his arms was in Vietnam, when the company he was in was charged with winning hearts and minds, which meant wrenching villagers from their homes in hamlets that were to be destroyed, relocating them in compounds where they were expected to re-create their lives with whatever they'd carried and whatever was on hand, Sam and other GIs helping the mothers by carrying their smallest children — the kids were mostly naked, he recounted to Oldman, and so thin, their bodies were as light as birds, you saw all their bones — but he doesn't mention this to June, just feels Luke's small body resting into him, feels his own limbs loosen, almost becomes drowsy because of the warmth thrown off by the fire and by the flames' mesmerizing effect. He shakes off his impulse to close his eyes, brings himself to comment on how strangely fire fascinates. Oldman claims it stirs something in us we can't quite remember, June replies quietly, something ancient that's born with us. Oldman, Sam says, resting his chin atop the boy's head as Luke reaches up, touches Sam's hair, is a remarkable man.

Have you known him a long time?

Just a few days.

Oh, she says.

Oldman is my friend, Luke remarks in great seriousness.

You're very lucky, Sam tells him. And the boy lets his hand wander, traces Sam's eyepatch, his scarred skin and shattered cheekbone, the face no one has touched since Rita, Sam unmoving beneath the child's gentle touch and immobile thereafter, June holding her breath, her tongue—she'd almost said *Luke, don't,* but thought better of it because Sam hadn't reacted, hadn't recoiled—until Luke drops his hand. When she found her voice, she asked if Sam wanted coffee or tea, but he said no thanks, it was nice to just sit in front of a fire, telling Luke that he didn't have a fireplace and that where he was from, most people didn't, then laughed when Luke responded, That's all right.

They sat for a long time without speaking. And maybe, June found herself thinking, this is what it could have been like had Ward not been who he was, if he had wanted the baby, if he had wanted to work things out and stay for Luke's sake: they could have managed the empty spaces between them, could have loved Luke if not each other; she'd never learned to be demanding, would never be because she saw herself as neutral, passive—it was safer that way, she'd learned that early on—and thought she could have been content to be unloved if only Ward had made a go of it for their child's sake. She can no longer remember exactly what Ward looked like, recalls him in a fractured way, knows his eyes were gray and that his chin was cleft, his hair straight, his fingertips blunt; there was a blue-black tattoo of a snake curled around a cross on his right forearm, but the whole of him is now beyond memory, for which she's become grateful, there's a softening to loss that occurs over time, people still living but gone fading away like the dead; and she gazes into the fire and thinks to summon the faces of those who've passed out of her life but can't, Auntie and her mother are shadows, June can't conjure them or Bo or his kind girl-friend or the college dropout. And she's never dreamed them; her dreams — when peopled, which is seldom — are of strangers she has never met, never known, who are oddly incidental and remain speechless and hold no meaning for her. Not unlike this stranger holding Luke, who's lost to his own thoughts, perhaps his own past; she has no way of knowing and doesn't ask and is pleased that he hasn't tried to engage her in any way, she doesn't know how she'd talk about what she was thinking, she's never known how to talk to any man but Oldman. When she finally stirs, she glances over at Luke, sees that he's asleep — how trans-lucent, how fine, a child's eyelids, a child's skin — and whispers: Let me take him from you, he must be heavy, but Sam shakes his head slightly, shushes her. And they remain like that, June in one armchair, the boy sleeping and Sam holding him in the other, the fire diminishing and the daylight waning, until Claire knocks on the door and opens it, enters before June is on her feet to flick on the light, closes the door behind her as Luke starts, squirms in Sam's arms, looks in surprise at the stranger who says: I've come to talk about Iris.

Luke slides off Sam's lap, stands beside him. Is she your grandma too?

No, Claire says, but I've known her all my life.

Me too.

I'm going to be staying with her for a while.

Why?

Because I want to.

Me too.

Me first, Claire tells him, and Luke frowns in confusion, leans back against Sam's thigh, looks at his mother. But Claire is already speaking quietly to June, not explaining the situation but stating simply that she—Claire—would appreciate June's cooperation, that what she—Claire—needs is for June to leave Iris to Claire. And, no, Claire can't say for how long. And, yes, she knows that Iris and Luke are together every morning; as a matter of fact, Iris has insisted on continuing to see the child although she's agreed to limit his visit to an hour each day, from ten to eleven. I'll come for him and bring him back, Claire tells her, beginning tomorrow.

And there's nothing I can do—

You could help Sam find his way to Oldman's—actually, Oldman said you'd be doing him a favor by having dinner there—and then guide him back here. Oldman will put my things in the car, Sam, to drop off here. I won't be needing the car, by the way.

And then Claire is gone, Sam rising and saying, Well, it's true, I could use some help finding my way to Oldman's if you wouldn't mind. And June wasn't sure whether she did; she was disturbed by Claire's brusque manner, felt threatened by this sudden interruption, perhaps even the cessation, of the rhythm her life—and Iris's, and Luke's—had, until this moment, flowed with. She barely recovered her equilibrium at Oldman's, despite the fact that he acted as though nothing were out of the ordinary, riposting that Sam, despite being a soup kitchen cook, was a natural, and that if he'd only stay he and Oldman would be able to work through, in the order in which they were presented, the 102 recipes in the Pilgrim cookbook Claire had given him. Enough recipes to see winter through, Oldman told Sam.

You can't be serious, came Sam's response. I mean, how long does winter last here?

A good while, Oldman said. Seriously, it's a monster you have to make room for, there's no keeping it at bay. Some years it snows and snows, and every year the cold seems deeper. Strange to say, I missed that in Europe. And Oldman went on, as they were eating, to tell them how stunned he'd been to find the French side of the English Channel verdant in winter, how the myth of Demeter and Persephone was stood on its head in that northern clime; not that it wasn't cold, there were the incessant rains, the damp, the winds, those buffeted clouds and wild seas, but no snow, no freeze, no likeness to the winters here. And Sam reflected aloud that it was hard to adjust in Nam, that there were the monsoons and then no rain at all—those were the seasons—but the worst was, there were no dawns or dusk, just twelve hours of light and then twelve of dark, with about two minutes of gray between the two.

Huh, Oldman commented. Claire said exactly the same thing.

She was there? Sam asked. And June noted the incredulous expression on Sam's face, the surprise in his voice, and for the first time wondered how well he and Claire knew each other.

On a junket for journalists, Oldman replied, organized by the powers that be to prove god knows what, that we were winning? that we weren't losing? Claire hated the whole show, chafed at having her hands tied, despised the patent propaganda, but at least it made her reconsider what she was doing, what she wanted to do, because toward the end of the tour they were herded into a U.S.-run hospital for the South Vietnamese—she described the place as jarring, because most everyone there, including kids, had terrible wounds, horrible burns, missing limbs—and that, she said, got her to thinking about tracking down GIs recuperating in VA hospitals around the country. No one was paying them much mind, and when her editors nixed her suggestion that the paper do a story on them, she decided to quit. And then went out on her own, taking the portraits that became her first solo exhibit, *War Wounded*. Which, actually, I thought was a terrible idea until I saw what she'd done. There's a dignity, a gravity—

I know what gravity is, Luke interrupted.

Luke, June interjected, it's not polite to speak when—

You do? Sam asked Luke.

It's why we don't go floating off into the air.

And why we fall down instead of up, Sam added, Oldman catching June's eye and June suddenly realizing that Sam was relieved by Luke's interruption, that his scars, that eyepatch, weren't the result of an accident, which is what she'd assumed, for she'd never met anyone who'd been in a war that hadn't started and ended before she was born. Oldman motioned for her to stay seated as he scraped his chair back and stood, began to clear the plates, but she rose as well and tousled her son's hair as he tried to best Sam by coming up with more and more outrageous examples of gravity's meaning, Sam relaxing back in his chair, Sam relaxed again, Sam suggesting that he and Luke take themselves into the other room unless Luke wanted to help with the dishes. Next time it'll be your turn, Oldman told the boy, and June said: Go on.

They worked side by side, June drying. Oldman finally asked whether Claire had spoken to her.

Not for very long. Only to say she'd be staying with Iris and wouldn't need my help.

You okay with that?

She shrugged, hesitated, confessed: A bit confused. I mean, she doesn't know how much help Iris actually needs. She didn't ask me that, didn't give me the chance to tell her.

Iris will tell her.

Iris doesn't always remember, Oldman. It's not just a matter of watching that she doesn't fall. Iris can mistake a tube of anything for toothpaste, and I'm not sure she can tell hot from cold unless she sees steam, and she can barely manage to be on her feet except with a walker or cane or someone to steady her; her balance is gone. Will she tell Claire that, will she say anything? We've never spoken about what I do for her, she's never asked anything of me, and if she doesn't tell —

Claire will manage. And she needs to be with Iris.

For how long?

I don't think she knows. Until certain things between them are settled. Or maybe just broached.

In the meanwhile, what should I do?

Just leave them alone. Maybe show Sam around, go for drives. He doesn't know the area, doesn't know anyone here.

I don't know him either. I couldn't possibly —

I've told Sam to suggest it.

She wiped her hands, placed the dish towel on a rack. I wouldn't know how to be with him, wouldn't know what to say.

Just be yourself.

June shook her head. Oldman reached for her wrists, held them, smiled. You'd be doing me — and Luke — a favor. With Sam around, the boy won't be upset at not being able to run off to Iris's a dozen times a day, and I'll be able to cook to my heart's content. It's not often I have a guest every evening, and I intend to take full advantage of the opportunity.

So he'll be staying with you.

He's more than welcome, especially now that Claire isn't here. I'd forgotten what it was like to have people stay, to hear footsteps and water running and feel someone else's presence, to look forward to long conversations in the evening and early-morning greetings. I know I'm being selfish, but I've considered that if you showed him around, he'd likely be steered back here evenings rather than elsewhere.

I'm sure he'd steer himself back, June said as Sam carried Luke into the kitchen, the boy's arms around Sam's neck and his head resting on Sam's shoulder. I think someone's tired, Sam said, but he shook his head as June approached, told her, I've got him. Oldman accompanied them to the car and put Claire's things into the trunk as Sam placed Luke in June's lap after seeing her into the car. Behind the wheel, he said, Don't tell me the way, and he drove silently through the night, navigating thoughtfully, taking his time, and June felt easy with the silence, the untrafficked going. He touched Luke's foot once, glancing at her, and she saw that he'd flipped the eyepatch up over his brow, glimpsed for the first time the enormity of the damage done to him, saw him fight the urge to duck his head, then turned his full attention again to the road. They didn't speak, and he didn't make one wrong turn. He pulled into Iris's drive and braked, readjusted the eyepatch, then let the engine idle with his hands on the wheel and not looking at her, just gazing straight ahead, finally taking a deep breath and exhaling, saying, So Oldman says that we — you, me and Luke — should go for a drive tomorrow.

And what do you say?

I'd like that very much.

Okay.

Okay, he echoed, cutting the engine and lights as Claire came through the door. He told June to wait as he got out, and Claire said she didn't need any help, hoisted her camera bag over a shoulder and carried her valise, half raised a hand in farewell before disappearing. He shut the trunk quietly, took Luke from June, and followed her into the garden and across a path illumined by the squares of light pooling through Iris's upstairs windows, June thinking *So Claire is staying upstairs, of course she must be,* realizing too how long it had been since Iris had moved into the downstairs bedroom and how June had missed the glow from that second floor, the way light seeped from the windows to spill ghostly shapes on the ground. The night was moonless, starless, and June didn't put on the porch light or the inside overhead, instead motioned for Sam to wait on the threshold as she went through the cottage and climbed into the loft and switched on a lamp next to her bed, then came down again, whereupon Sam placed the boy on the daybed. They undid the laces of his shoes, and she crooked Luke's knees and rolled him onto his side and covered him with an afghan throw. Sam stood close to her, perhaps too close, for as she straightened she brushed against him and they each took a step back from the other, June bringing her hands behind her back and Sam standing with hands dangling, pensive, as if about to speak, and then Claire was at the door they hadn't shut and Sam moved, herded her away from the porch and back to Iris's house, their voices low and their heads bent toward each other when they stopped, June watching their hands meet as Claire passed him what June later realized were keys before Claire disappeared into the darkness of Iris's downstairs and closed the door behind

her. Sam turned back toward the cottage, halted before June on
its porch, looked off and then at her, looked at his feet, shuffled
a bit. So, he finally said, how's noon tomorrow?

Good, she said.

Good, he echoed. And then he moved toward June, placed
his unscarred cheek against one side of her unblemished face for
a second, two, before straightening and telling her good night.

Iris

ALTHOUGH IRIS CHAFED at having Luke for only an hour each morning and missed June, she didn't say as much to Claire. There was something in the way Claire watched her with the boy that made Iris suspect her daughter wondered whether Iris had ever been as loving with her, and Iris was not unaware that Claire was methodically rummaging through the upstairs each night after Iris went to bed and was, supposedly, asleep: but sleep did not claim her easily now that she wasn't alone, although Iris did not mention that either. And had decided she wouldn't, even if she could have said whether she suffered sleeplessness because she'd been alone for so many years that she was now incapable of adjusting to anyone else's footfalls and rustlings and breathing, or whether her insomnia and intermittent wakefulness were specifically caused by Claire's undeniable and intense presence.

She merely told Claire, after several days of her daughter's company, that she saw no reason for her to continue staying with her. They'd seen each other. Iris had said what she'd wanted to tell Claire in person: *All of this, everything I have will be yours, but I've altered my will slightly and left something to June and the boy. Duncan—who will, of course, be the executor of the estate—has a copy for you.* That, and: *Until you sell the place—which is what I expect you'll do—please allow June to continue living in the cottage, if she so chooses, in return for keeping up this house and the garden.* And: *There'll be no funeral: Duncan has instructions as to how to dispose of my ashes.*

Claire made no response, just studied Iris silently with those dark eyes and inscrutable gaze that disturbed. Iris suspected it masked either calculation or consternation, and so decided to say more than she had. I am going to die soon, to my own relief, she informed Claire, and I'll die here. I will not consider going into a nursing home or abide help here, I don't want strangers in my house, it's enough that June watches over my deterioration without making a fuss.

And if I stayed, Claire said.

You have no reason to. You never did.

And Claire didn't tell Iris *I had a reason, I had the only reason I ever needed, but Duncan wouldn't say the word;* instead, she replied evenly: Actually, I do. I want to talk about Matthew.

I don't, Iris said, and I won't.

There was no rejoinder Claire could or would make. But she didn't leave, and Iris grudgingly grew used to her presence—which was so unlike June's; that girl was like a shadow, ethereal—and remained stalwart in her struggle to get through each day, to do as much as she could on her own, not protesting when Claire began to photograph, document, Iris's rising and dressing, her use of the walker, her tremors, the way soup spilled from her spoon, the way food dribbled from her mouth, the way she slumped for long hours in an armchair facing the garden she could no longer walk through, walk into, work in. Claire did not spare Iris her privacy: she followed Iris into the bathroom, photographing her while she sat beneath the shower in a plastic chair to wash and rinse herself; and Iris succumbed to this intrusion, she who had never before been naked before her daughter. The beads of water pained Iris, and she pitied her now long-unfamiliar body, with its wasted muscles and large joints — Claire saw her mother's shoulder blades and hips as angular protrusions seemingly about to break through skin; her spine as an unevenly strung set of knobs pushing out — and her planed belly, flattened chest, those tremulous limbs, gnarled with veins, that had become thinner than her elbows and knees. Nude, Iris no longer recognized, refused to recognize, herself, and so it did not matter that Claire witnessed and recorded the most private ritual left to her, for hidden from Claire's lens were the pain and Iris's self-pity. These, Iris kept safe within her.

Only Iris's hair — its autumn-oak-leaf color faded but still visible beneath those predominant silver streaks — was still luxurious, had retained its thickness and heft, incongruous given the obvious vulnerability of her dying body. Luke always reached up and touched it as Iris read to him, the child leaning back against her chest, or, facing her when they talked, gently played with it or pushed it behind her ears. Claire began to photograph them together too, and Iris never knew whether that kept Claire from asking whether Iris had ever been as loving with her. Iris never asked whether Claire remembered being held and caressed, whether she remembered what Iris considered their happiest times, on vacation at Mabel's without Matthew and at home when Claire was very young, before Matthew became obsessed with trussing not only himself but also Iris, using chains and locks and cords and ropes and leaving her tied to bedposts or immobile and twisted on her stomach or side with her wrists and ankles tied behind her back, claiming he was only trying to make Iris over in his own image as an escape artist. He changed as his power over Iris grew, he came to revel in his realization that she could not undo those knots he tied or those locks he locked, that she could not escape him, would not ever; and slowly, almost methodically, he pushed at that tenuous boundary separating bondage from sadism, satiating himself with his prowess over her, and—upon that one occasion when Iris somehow summoned the courage to resist him—finally threatening to instead turn his attentions to Claire, who was then five, and teach her to become a contortion and escape artist, a child magician and wonder. Which Iris would never allow, and so succumbed once again and of course thereafter to what Matthew had come to sneeringly call his artistry, continuing to suffer what he made Iris do to him, what he made her watch him do to himself, what he—often violently—did to her. Because Iris so feared Matthew's intentions toward their daughter, she kept her husband from Claire by sacrificing herself to his every desire, swearing to herself that the child would thereby never experience his obsessions or perversities; and she did all, everything, that was necessary to keep Claire from him, and from herself, encouraging her daughter to find refuge in books and being amazed that, even as a child, Claire preferred those that had photographs of people staring back at or walking away from the camera, who at any rate remained on the page and did not demand anything more than Claire's gaze; and now, Iris reflected, perhaps that was how her daughter became self-sufficient and insular, made her peace with the world as an outsider, and eventually came to frame what she saw to her own peculiar satisfaction. Yes, she had, Iris told herself, saved Claire from that dark, lithe man Claire so resembled that people who knew them always remarked *She's the spitting image of her father,* which is why after Matthew's death Iris couldn't bring herself to look upon her daughter.

Whether Claire had minded, Iris will never ask. Although the question that had long ago stopped gnawing at her had once again come to mind because of Claire's presence, Luke dispelled it by crawling onto Iris's lap each morning for that hour Claire allowed. And no matter what they read together, the hour didn't end without Luke excitedly talking about the snow to come, Iris chiming in that she wanted that first snowfall to be heavy so Luke could make a snowman for her in front of her patio while she watched from inside the house, the two of them discussing what Luke would use for the snowman's eyes and nose and mouth and arms, whether the snowman would wear a hat and scarf. Claire listened to and photographed them during these conversations, when both were at their most animated planning this snowman, until the morning Luke interrupted Claire with: How come you're always taking pictures of me and Grandma?

So I can give them to you, so you'll know what you looked like as a kid after you grow up. So you'll know what your grandma looked like then. So you won't forget.

I don't know how to do that yet, Luke told her.

He won't forget, Iris said. And neither will I.

Okay, Claire replied, then let's say I'm taking pictures because your grandma is my project. At which Luke frowned, studying Claire in great seriousness, his mouth pursed. Enough, Iris told Claire. And Claire acquiesced, put her camera down and stepped away, then returned a few minutes later and tapped her wrist: time for Luke to go. Iris watched him run across to the cottage, where he and June would wait for Claire's friend, who now came every day and took them off, away, until after nightfall; and when Claire's friend—Claire hadn't mentioned his name, and Iris did not ask—arrived, Iris watched him walk over to the cottage and knock on its door and scoop the boy up in his arms, kiss him and set him down, greet June by touching his cheek to hers, then pocket his hands before walking June and Luke back across the garden, before walking them out of Iris's life for—to Iris—the rest of yet another interminable day.

Another interminable night too, during which Iris will not take a sleeping pill or the antispasmodic she terms a muscle re-laxer, and so during which she will twilight-sleep and wake to hear Claire's quiet, insistent rummaging. Iris knew Claire was going through every drawer, every closet, every page of every book, looking for any remnant of Iris's life, for postcards, notes, letters, any photograph that had escaped Iris's destruction; but Iris had destroyed everything that could have reminded her of Matthew, those years spent with him. Iris would never men-tion that she now believed she had—tragically, perhaps, and certainly pitiably—with this disease suffered a physical man-ifestation of the emotional state she'd suffered after his death when she had determined to face no one, to turn herself inward, away from the world and from Claire. She also knew that if she spoke of Matthew, if she would, if Claire would—Claire had never spoken of her father to Iris before, and Iris would never know that Claire had spoken of him only once to Duncan, having been asked her reaction to having learned, months after Matthew was buried and finally from Mabel that he was dead, simply stating *He terrified me*—if they, Iris and Claire, would speak of him, discuss him, nothing would change, for nothing between her and Claire would ever change.

This visit can't go on indefinitely, Iris finally admitted to herself. And the next morning said coldly to Claire, with no further explanation or protestation: I'm not used to having company at night.

Me neither, came Claire's response.

Mabel

MABEL WAS SURPRISED but hid her disappointment: neither Claire nor June and Luke were at Iris's. Claire, Iris told her, had gone to have lunch with Duncan and would later that afternoon visit with Oldman, and June and Luke were with a friend of Claire's who came by every noon and took them away. Where, Iris didn't know.

Mabel made tea and brought it to the table, readied the cups, and watched Iris stand from the armchair and then maneuver her walker over to Mabel and manage to sit across from her. When Iris had called, she'd surprised Mabel by asking whether Mabel had any photographs from those summers during which Iris and Claire stayed at the cabins, or from the school year during which Claire remained with Mabel and Paul. Roland had helped Mabel go through several shoeboxes of keepsakes from the attic; it had been difficult enough for her to finally clear out Paul's clothes by herself, handle them knowing that they'd been laundered before he'd left that last time, that they bore no trace of his scent, so the most she could do was remove them from the hangers and fold them, smooth them, pack them carefully into boxes, then take those boxes some seventy miles away and in a largish town donate his belongings to charity.

Roland had helped her go through the photographs, but he hadn't retrieved them from the attic, where Mabel had finally decided to put Paul's shoes, which she couldn't bring herself to throw out. She sat on the attic floor in front of them for a long time, hugging her knees; the way he'd worn them was still visible, each heel worn down toward the inside of each foot, the last trace of Paul's having been alive, of the way he'd walked and stood and danced. His two pair of dress shoes were polished, his loafers scuffed, his broken-in work boots laced with new cords, his leather boots treated with beeswax. Size eleven and a half: a big man. His laugh and heart bigger, the way he'd loved her beyond measure. The way she'd loved him.

He would have wanted her to be happy, and she was. She marveled at that, marveled at Roland's constancy, at how different he was from Paul; and perhaps that was what had made life with Roland possible, for the two bore no resemblance to each other in personality or physique, Paul big and bearlike and loud and funny with his freewheeling ways, a man who commanded attention just by entering a crowded room because of his size and booming voice and love of storytelling and laughter, whereas Roland was slender and soft-spoken and reflective, a man who blended in with walls or quietly slipped onto a barstool without being noticed and who walked beaches solo in a never-ending quest to find what he hadn't yet found or see what he'd often seen, perfectly content to take the measure of the shore, the dunes, and content to weather those years of bachelorhood through which he'd waited out his time without impatience, like a sailor untroubled by the doldrums because soothed by the lifeless sails and quiet surface of the sea. Paul the tornado, Roland the calm, having nothing in common except that each had become, would always be, a part of her life.

Iris had been right: Roland never asked, just one day told her: Marry me. And she thought then as she knew now that Paul would have wanted her to be happy. After a while she stopped hugging her knees and left Paul's shoes where they were, where she wanted them to always remain, and brought the boxes down from the attic, went through the photographs with Roland, and for Iris. Or, rather, for Claire: after all, Iris had said, I'm asking for Claire, I destroyed everything that was here, everything she keeps searching for, and the longer she comes up empty-handed the longer she'll stay with me, use me as her excuse—she claims I'm her project—and photograph me constantly, no matter what I'm doing or mostly not doing, run interference with my life. I'm at my wits' end, Mabel, because Claire wants or needs something I can't give her, which maybe you can. And which I'd appreciate.

They'd found Brownie and Polaroid prints. The shoebox Mabel had brought with her sat on the table's far end from Iris, who did not want to look at what it contained. There's one of you in a polka-dot two-piece bathing suit standing next to me, Mabel told Iris, and I'm wearing that striped one-piece; and there's another of Claire in that bathing suit that was gathered in tucks; she's sitting on that plaid blanket you had and wearing barrettes shaped like flowers. Are you sure you don't want to see just these two?

Iris shook her head. I don't need to be nostalgic, she told Mabel. Actually, I'm not even capable of such a thing. And I'm not interested in seeing myself as someone I can no longer recognize.

Mabel herself had barely recognized Iris as she now was, had been shocked at her friend's appearance—it was as though she were already a corpse, her skin wan and discolored by an unhealthy sheen and drawn tightly over bones and joints, the backs of her hands, her hollow face—and at the violence of her tremors. That she leaned tremulously into her hands on the walker and managed to shuffle and scuff about seemed both miraculous and tragic. She appeared to be on the verge of utter exhaustion, but she continued to speak, telling Mabel—with a hint of that irony Mabel knew Iris was capable of—that despite not being interested in seeing herself, she had also begun to hallucinate. In flashes, Iris said, fish will fly through the garden, small creatures scamper across the floor, bats hang in ceiling corners just for an instant before they're gone. Funny how they're not there at all, but I can't help but notice them.

Iris shrugged in the ensuing silence—Mabel didn't know what to say—then sighed, Claire is tiresome.

You mean tired.

No. Yes. Well, both. Both. She hovers, usually with that camera in her hand, while I'm awake. Searches through the upstairs after I'm in bed. She wanted to talk about Matthew, but I won't. Someday after I'm gone, she will probably tell you the same.

I wouldn't know what to say about him.

You should tell her that I hated him.

Iris—

Grew to hate him, grew to hate the man who, in social situations, was the one I'd fallen in love with but who, in private, became more and more of a monster. Was a monster. Everyone thought he was the life of the party, but no one knew what he was like, that our marriage was perfect on the outside and rotten within. He was sick, Mabel. He sickened me. I couldn't leave or divorce him, for what would people say; no one divorced in those days, except for adultery or extreme cruelty, and I couldn't, no, wouldn't air our dirty laundry in public and, after all, we were Catholic. I could never bring myself to tell anyone, not even a priest—anyway, I'd dropped out of the fold, stopped going to church when my marriage descended into hell—what life with him was like: the ropes, chains, masks, whips, gloves, eventually those obscene leather outfits, eventually my horror and humiliation. Every couple I knew seemed happy, *normal,* and we seemed happy, normal, but I was at my wits' end because of him, because I was living a lie; and we had Claire, I was supposed to love her, I *did* love her, but I had to learn to keep her at arm's length to protect her. The only way he'd stay away from Claire was if I didn't divide my attention, if he remained the center of my world, if I gave him what he wanted, did what he said. The only times I could breathe, remember what it was to be happy, was when I could get away from him, come to your place; and I dreaded returning to him, knowing the worst would begin all over again. There were times I thought I'd go insane. And then he died the way he did—it wasn't the first time he'd strung himself up, the strangling excited him sexually, he thrilled to almost die, thrilled too in escaping death—and I was mortified, for the police and coroner knew how he'd killed himself, the priest had been informed, it was all I could do to pull strings to get his death ruled accidental, to get him buried in hallowed ground for the sake of keeping up appearances. And of course word got out anyway, everyone knew, and even if they didn't, I knew I'd never again be able to hold my head up. I grew to hate Matthew in life, and I hated him in death: he ruined me from both sides of the grave. My only consolation, the only thing I could do, was to erase every trace of him. Tell Claire, if she ever asks you, that that's why I destroyed everything he'd ever touched, every blade of grass he ever walked upon; it's why I had this house and the cottage and the garden ripped apart and redone. Why I burned or threw away everything else. That the only thing I couldn't cart away or erase was Claire, whom I couldn't look at and so turned my back on. To save her, and to save my sanity.

Iris, Mabel said thoughtfully after a long moment—watching Iris watch her and not reading anguish or any other emotion in that rigid skull, those receding eyes—Claire would never ask me.

I think she might. One day or another she might want to know why I kept her at arm's length while he was alive, why she and I lived separate lives after he died. Not that it excuses what happened—that is, everything that never happened—between us. And not that either of us is sorry.

I can't imagine you're not. That she's not.

Iris shrugged again. She seemed happy, Iris said, she had Duncan to watch over her—which he did well—and, of course, she found Oldman. She left and made her way in the world.

And Mabel, who could not say this was untrue, studied this woman with whom she'd been friends for much of her life and realized how impossible it is to know the inner workings of another's being: Iris had divulged more than Mabel had ever suspected, had divulged more than she'd ever expected, for she'd suspected and expected nothing. She'd brought the photographs, and the certainty came over her that she'd never see Iris again, that this visit was her last, that Iris had used the photographs—which she indeed wanted for Claire—to summon Mabel, that the farewell about to take place would do so between the living, that there'd be no opportunity or reason to say anything to Iris after she was dead.

Mabel poured more tea, but neither of them touched her cup. They sat in silence for a long time, during which Mabel wondered what would become of June, of Luke; without them, the cottage seemed forlorn, the way this house, she reflected, once Iris was gone, would seem to June and Luke, deserted during the day, dark and desolate during the night. Mabel and Roland were going to let go of the cabins—they'd closed early this season, her last, she and Roland would put the place up for sale in the spring—and even if this weren't the case, Mabel wouldn't be able to offer June what Iris had, a permanency, what knowledge of planting and pruning and reaping Iris had shared, this garden where Duncan would—unbeknown to anyone, even Claire—scatter Iris's ashes of fine and coarse powder and pieces of bone upon the snow that would be covered by another snowfall and by those following, and then melt into the ground with spring's thaw.

Mabel cleared her throat, decided to ask what might happen to June but saw that Iris's chin had dipped, that she was dozing, her eyelids translucent and the eyes behind them restless as though searching through dream. And so she asked nothing, instead quietly rose and cleared the table, washed and rinsed the teapot and cups and saucers, the spoons. She took her seat again and watched Iris sleep, was grateful for the almost indiscernible rise and fall of her thin chest, and waited. When Iris finally opened her eyes, Mabel managed a smile.

I've kept you far too long, Iris told her.

I'll come again.

Please don't.

You're sure.

There's no sense in it. No reason. You've seen enough, and I've asked more than enough of you: perhaps too much. For which I'm sorry.

Don't be, Mabel told her. And at that Iris reached for the walker, pulled herself up and stood shakily, shuffled toward the door. The cloudcover was heavy, solid, the day's wane settling. Mabel followed Iris, then stepped around her to let herself out. Iris stared across the garden as the chill hit them both.

Goodbye, she said.

Mabel kissed her, held her face in her hands. Oh, Iris—

Tell me, Iris whispered, are you happy?

Yes. Yes. Are you?

I will be, Iris told her. Soon, finally, I will be.

Oldman

DUNCAN BROUGHT the hot toddies from his apartment upstairs and set them on his office desk. Oldman leaned forward in his chair and cupped his hands around his toddy — he'd not worn gloves despite the sudden shift in weather on this windy day in which the temperatures would barely climb to the low forties, and the Studebaker's heater wasn't working. Before they'd taken a second sip, June and Sam and Luke came through the door, as they'd done the previous Friday, to collect her stipend. They didn't linger, and Duncan commented after they'd left that June seemed to stand taller, had a certain radiance that altered what he'd always considered to be her plainness, indeed glowed in a way he'd never thought imaginable. As if, he continued, Sam had cast a spell. It looks to be pretty much mutual, Oldman agreed, although I like to think I had something to do with easing Sam out of the hell he'd pretty much kept himself in. I mean, Oldman continued, that first night at my place, he fell apart, just began to sob, and I bet it was the first time he'd grieved in front of anyone since the day the world blew up on him. And I didn't know him, didn't know anything about him other than what Claire said, that he was a friend, and about the only thing we knew of each other was what we saw in our faces. I told him mine had been scarred by a monkey, and suddenly I had no idea what I had on my hands because he just went to pieces, with me sitting there listening, watching, letting him go on, and hoping this wouldn't end badly. That I wasn't going be facing another David Jennings. Lord, remember him?

How could I forget? Duncan replied: and who in town didn't remember the Jennings boy, who'd come back from Nam sporting a Mohawk and earrings but hadn't—aside from wearing only fatigues and combat boots and speaking of nothing but how much fun he'd had as a sniper, sitting in trees and shooting people he called gooks—shown signs of derangement immediately upon his return, although some weeks later word began to spread that he'd canvassed every bar in town looking for anyone who'd ever hunted or owned a gun and was willing to pay him whatever they thought the privilege of stalking and shooting him was worth, the caveat being that they had to pay up front and take their chances that their skills couldn't match his, since—he boasted, probably with reason—he knew how to cover his tracks. And when he had no takers, he became more adamant, going so far as to offer to bet on the outcome, both parties putting in equal amounts into a third party's hands, say, David Jennings had suggested, Duncan's, with whom he and his family had never had any dealings but whose reputation as an honest man equaled Oldman's, the difference being that Duncan was not—unlike Oldman—apt to visit the Jennings family

upon hearing such a thing. Which Oldman did, under the mis-
apprehension that the boy's parents and siblings knew what their
son and brother was trying to wrangle any takers into, which
they didn't, and they lost no time and minced no words inform-
ing Oldman that he, Oldman, was talking nonsense. For David
Jennings, his family believed, was a fine boy; not only that, he
had medals and an honorable discharge to prove it, and the U.S.
government wasn't idiotic, it took care of its soldiers and recognized valor for what it was, so Oldman should take his anti-
war sympathies—which the Jennings family obviously thought
extended to David, who'd given his all—elsewhere, and fast.
The irony, of course, was that Oldman, about a month after that
hapless visit to the Jennings family, whom he considered even
more idiotic than the U.S. government, was the one who convinced the town's sheriff and deputies not to shoot the Jennings
boy, who was armed, most likely dangerous, and perched high
within the foliage of one of the oak trees that graced the town's
main street, and it was Oldman who eventually talked the former sniper down by promising that every man and woman
in town—none of whom was standing around, everyone taking cover except the law, who were crouched on the far side of
the sheriff's car, and Oldman and Duncan—had changed their
minds about not wanting to hunt him down. All Jennings had
to do was climb down and start over, play the game the way he
said it should be, that Oldman would match his bet and let him
take off and try to cover his tracks with a quarter-hour head
start.

So David Jennings, carrying a rifle mounted with a tele-
scope strapped to his shoulder, swung out of that tree with the
ease of an acrobat and got himself tackled before his feet hit
the ground by the sheriff—who, despite being somewhat cor-

pulent, was more agile than most big men and hadn't forgotten his high school football years—and was shackled and safely escorted to the local hospital, where he was sedated, and where the local authorities signed the papers Duncan helped prepare that remanded the Jennings boy to a VA hospital's psychiatric ward, where he remained a good while. And Oldman got himself thanked by the town council as well as cursed by the Jennings family who—shocking, this, Oldman had quipped to Duncan later, much later, when enough time had passed to allow for jokes—wouldn't consider the fact that the outcome could have been much, much worse.

Anyway, Oldman told Duncan, the two of them relaxing back with their hands cupped around their toddies, Sam broke down and all I could think of was I didn't know this man from Adam—I mean, at least with the Jennings boy I'd known what was going on—and that if I only kept plying him with alcohol, at one point he'd have to fall over. But the more he drank and wept and talked, the more convinced I became that he'd never bared his soul to anyone before, and that he was both harmless and a lot more deeply scarred than what I was looking at.

And is he?

Well, from what he's told me over the last few weeks, he was. And now.

And now, well, I'd say he's considering that it might be possible to put the past in perspective and get on with his life, do something more than cook for a soup line, maybe come back here and give small-town life a try.

Duncan raised his eyebrows, queried: And stay with you?

No, Oldman replied. No, he repeated slowly, that would complicate matters. Because, Duncan, I've been thinking of asking June to move in with me. To offer her and the boy a home after Iris passes. I know—Oldman raised a hand, stopped Duncan from interrupting—about Iris's will, I know the financial provision she's made for June; Claire's told me. Told me Iris's wishes as well, in terms of letting June stay on.

Well, at least I don't have to invoke lawyer-client privilege.

And it wouldn't have mattered if Claire hadn't told me. Because once Iris is gone, it'd be hard for the girl to continue on there, raising Luke alone. I'm not getting any younger—

You're not serious, Oldman, Duncan interjected, rolling his empty glass between his palms, don't tell me you're thinking of proposing—

Oldman laughed, shaking his head. I want her to legally become my daughter, Duncan, which would stop wagging tongues as to what our relationship might be. I want her and Luke to have a home.

And provide you with a family.

I never said I wasn't selfish. And I surely always wanted one.

Have you mentioned this to her?

Not yet. I needed to know if the law would allow it.

The law would, but—

You don't need to caution me, Duncan. I've never done anything on impulse.

Except talk crazy people down from trees.

I was being extremely thoughtful in that situation, but awfully quick at it, as I was trying to avoid possibly being among those who were going to be shot at.

Well, if June is willing, I'll do the paperwork. But I think she has the right to know what Iris has allowed for before making her decision.

I agree.

Damn it, Oldman, you're supposed to argue the point.

I can't. I've asked Claire—who doesn't know what I'm proposing here—to tell June about Iris's will and wishes before she and Sam leave.

Which is when?

Oldman considered Duncan quizzically. I thought Claire would have told you: the day after tomorrow.

Whoa, Duncan said.

They've been here for almost three weeks. Claire's moving back to my place this evening after she talks to June about Iris's will. I'm surprised Claire didn't tell you over lunch.

Lunch turned out to be a bit awkward.

Because of Meredith?

Most likely, Duncan said. Did not say, *I couldn't face Claire alone, I didn't want to confront or evade that question of whether I'm spoken for, and who knows whether Claire took Meredith as my answer or simply my shield.* Not that it wasn't pleasant, Duncan went on, only quite impersonal. I handed Claire an envelope containing a copy of Iris's will and codicil, and then we made small talk and ate and went our separate ways. She hasn't come by or called. I had no idea she was going to speak to June.

Who will be mostly shocked by the fact that Iris is going to die sooner rather than later, I fear, Oldman confided. I don't think she's understood that. Young people are very good at ignoring—or not recognizing—mortality. I'm assuming this will hit her hard, and then, a few days on, she'll begin to worry over what it will be like after Iris is gone.

Which is when you'll offer her—

Everything I can.

And what if Sam returns to sweep her off her feet?

Well, that would be fine with me, I couldn't wish for a better son-in-law, but he isn't one to rush things. He's told me he won't leave the soup kitchen in the lurch, that he wants to return with enough money to settle himself, stand on his own two feet while trying to make a go of it here, that he doesn't want to hang on by the skin of his teeth after renting an apartment and before finding a job. Sam is a cautious man. And even if he weren't, June is incapable of being swept off her feet. She made that mistake once and suffered immensely for it.

Love makes people erratic, Oldman.

Can, but doesn't always. Some, it just makes true to themselves, and to others.

Duncan paused, studied his empty glass, knew that Oldman realized he'd inadvertently hit a raw nerve. For love had never made Duncan erratic or true to himself; he'd shrugged off being the most sought-after bachelor during his first and much of his second decade in town, only occasionally dating and never having what could be construed or misconstrued as a steady relationship until Meredith came into his life and remained resolute, having what Oldman considered the patience of Job and who, Oldman also considered, had probably finally come very close to winning Duncan over by sheer steadfastness, that conviction she held evident that Duncan was a man worth his salt even if he had to be accepted on the strangest terms, which had so far extended to never formalizing any emotional relationship. For he'd had that once as Claire's legal guardian, and—as Oldman suspected, but would never know—he'd suffered his role as such, had never once trespassed the boundaries of that role, and had kept Claire on the other side of the line he'd drawn, which line—as Oldman also suspected, but also would never know—Claire had had no respect for; indeed, she'd constantly tested its inviolability, had continued until now to question whether Duncan still felt bound by what had from the beginning legally defined their relationship.

Look, Duncan finally said, I'm not much of an expert when it comes to love. But I will point out that legal adoption won't guarantee June will live with you for any length of time, never mind stay with you forever. Don't count on either.

All I'm counting on is my intuition, Oldman admitted, thinking, as he often had since meeting June, of her double, the young woman he'd once found atop a rubble pile and fallen in love with and left behind, lost. *And causality,* he thought to himself.

Well, Duncan pronounced after a moment, I believe June will be as honest with you as you are with her. Just let her know what your expectations are, what strings might be attached. Don't keep those in the back of your mind.

I expect only to give her a choice—and, if she chooses, security and love for both her and Luke—and beyond that, my only hope is that she'll decide how to live her life as she sees fit. There won't be any strings, there's no reason for any: it's *June* we're talking about.

I haven't lost sight of that.

I'll be taking this slow, Duncan. I'm not even sure when I'll bring any of this up to her.

In the meanwhile, what would you like me to do?

Wait, Oldman said. Join me and Claire and Sam for dinner tomorrow night.

Waiting's easy, but, sorry, I can't make dinner.

I meant to include Meredith. Bring her along.

Actually, she's out of town for a few days. And I have other plans.

Are you about to lock yourself away?

At the moment, I'm about to fix myself another toddy.

Fix two, Oldman told him.

Duncan

HE HEARD THE KNOCK he'd already decided to ignore, the knock Duncan had known, feared, would come: he'd called Oldman's too late, they'd had an early dinner, Claire had taken her car and was gone, and Oldman didn't know when she'd be back; she'd gone out late the night before and had returned just before dawn, telling Oldman that she wanted to take advantage of the only two free nights she now had, hoping to transfix whatever wildlife might step out into the sweep of the headlights; maybe Duncan could call around seven the next morning, Oldman had suggested, for they'd be up, Sam and Claire planned to leave by eight. Will do, Duncan said, and then he'd put down the receiver and pulled down the shades and turned off the lights and sat in the dark. He hadn't expected Claire to be insistent — how could he have forgotten that streak of determination? — and listened to the knocking grow louder, more emphatic, heard the door rattle and reverberate, until he was convinced she was using both fists and would likely pound through the wood never mind wake the entire main street. She must have been eyeing the upstairs apartment windows, for it was only when Duncan turned on a lamp that she ceased banging and instead began again to politely and quietly knock.

He went downstairs and, without turning the lights on in his office, opened the door a crack.

Duncan, she said.

Claire.

She looked to her left and right, put her hands on her hips. You can let me in, she told him. He hesitated, then did, and she slipped past him and didn't stop in the office but headed up the stairs, which she'd never before climbed, and walked into his apartment, in which that one lamp cast a dull light. She didn't pause or look around, just stripped off her jacket and dropped it beside the armchair Duncan had been seated in. It's almost ten, he said, turning on another lamp, and she looked at him with an amused gaze. Rum? he queried. Neat, she answered. He went into another room and returned with two drinks, sat opposite her, listened to her tell him that, to her amazement, she'd been able to photograph Sam that afternoon as he and Oldman came up through the pasture. Oldman had been leading the pony—you know how he always says the creature is fickle and always adds, *What pony isn't*—and Sam had Oldman's horse, and the two were in deep discussion. And it struck me, she said, that that's how it should be, Oldman should always have company, his house is too big for one person and after all the man's not getting any younger. Oldman had told Claire that he'd finally decided to retire from those Saturday evenings he spent at the town newspaper's darkroom, he was thinking of retiring from his every involvement with the town and intended to hand that torch to Duncan because it wasn't like half the town didn't drop in on Duncan anyway; and what with winter coming on—Oldman said he hated to admit it, but even if this winter came off mild he probably wouldn't think so, it'd *seem* harder than any that came before, given the care he had to give those foolish equines and useless curs and his place—it had dawned on him that he didn't want to face the season and indeed the rest of his life alone. He went on to confide to Claire that he was, eventually, going to suggest to June that she and Luke move in with him, and that the only other person who knew this was Duncan. Oldman then went on to say that he hadn't decided to take this step only because he'd taken June under his wing, but also because she'd acted toward him as a daughter, and because she was quiet and plainspoken and self-contained and appreciative, and because he adored Luke. They were already, he considered, his surrogate family: and that had surprised Claire. More surprising, she told Duncan, was that as the two men were leading that pony and horse toward her and the barn, it struck her that Sam was the likely candidate to be the son, should Oldman want to round out the family.

At any rate, they saw her raise her camera as they neared, and Sam—who'd once told her *No photographs* in no uncertain terms—didn't protest, didn't make any motion to deny her. You know, she continued, what fine heads that horse and pony have, but beyond this they're nothing alike, in contrast to Oldman and Sam who bear such a strange resemblance to each other—both lean, about the same height, and scarred—despite the difference in their ages, and despite Sam's eyepatch. They both knew what I was doing, she went on, but it was Oldman who worked magic, drawing close and stopping and waiting, knowing those

critters would immediately become impatient and start toss-
ing their heads, rolling their eyes; and then the sun's rays broke
through the clouds and streaked down in the background, and
Oldman kept talking to Sam and got him to look up at the camera, cutting short his one protestation with *Hell, why not, son?*
We're the best-looking men in this field.

You can't imagine what it was like, she told Duncan, click-
ing that shutter as Sam looked directly at her and Oldman
turned in three-quarters profile to scold the pony that had begun to nip at the horse, Sam looking at the camera with that
patch and slight frown, as if unaware that the pony's upper lip
was raised and its teeth bared and that the horse was rearing
its head. This, she said, is the photograph Oldman will hang in
his museum room alongside those tintypes and old farm implements. It's the one I'll frame and give to Sam as a keepsake of the
day he relented, having realized because of his time with Oldman that it's never the scars which can be seen that matter.

And it was as if, Duncan realized, Claire had never left:
she'd slipped off her shoes and curled into that armchair and
commanded his attention because of her mere presence, never
mind that voice he'd so missed, that chiseled face, the shape of
her hands, neck, her shoulders. He has no photograph of her,
has never seen one; even Claire's high school yearbook had a
blank frame rather than a portrait. So, he said slowly, you think
this keepsake will matter to Sam.

As a reminder of that moment and its meaning, yes.

Duncan went into the other room and returned with the
bottle of rum, poured her another shot, poured himself one. As
Sam intends to return, Duncan said, he'll likely be spending a
lot of time with Oldman.

But he and Oldman will never recapture that moment in the same way as my photograph.

Memory can be powerful.

Or distorted, or empty. Claire brushed her hand through the air, stopped Duncan from responding. Duncan, I spent every night at Iris's searching through the upstairs of her house, going through every book, every drawer, every closet, that attic, every nook and cranny, hoping to find something, anything — a picture, a handwritten note, a letter — that might have survived from my childhood. It must have disturbed Iris, though she never said, for the day you and I — and Meredith — had lunch I returned to find that Mabel, who'd visited Iris the same day, had brought and left — surely at Iris's request — a shoebox half filled with photographs of us. Of me, of Iris, sometimes of the three of us. The shock was, I hadn't remembered, didn't remember, Iris as she'd been before she withdrew from the world; what shocked me more is, I realized I was photographing Iris every day while staying with her — recording everything she did, her every expression and gesture — because I don't and can't remember what Iris actually looked like during my childhood, not even in the following years when I lived in the cottage. And what she looks like now bears no resemblance to the woman in those photographs. Not only was she beautiful, but she was also somehow *animated* in those stills, there's laughter behind her smile, amusement in her eyes; I could see how supple and graceful she was, imagine her walking or dancing or swimming out of those frames. Those photographs are now all I have of *then,* in contrast to all I have of *now.* But the in-between, well, what of that? Who *was* she?

Someone, Duncan pronounced slowly, who wanted to forget.

He saw the quizzical, incisive look on Claire's face, watched her sip the rum, anticipated the question he knew would not remain unspoken. He braced himself, felt oddly, slightly drunk.

And was that possible? Claire asked. Were you able to forget, was I, as much as we tried?

Duncan emptied his glass, reached for the rum and poured another two fingers, shook his head, sighed. *Admit it,* he told himself, but the most he managed was: At times I've missed you, Claire.

She got to her feet, walked over to him. Don't hog that rum, she warned, taking the bottle from him, pouring herself another shot, taking a sip, studying him the while. Get up, she said, putting her glass down, taking his glass from him. When he stood he met the hand she'd raised as if to dance, felt her other hand on the back of his shoulder, encircled her waist with his free arm. Claire—

You owe me this dance, Duncan. It was the only promise you ever broke.

And she stepped in to him, rested her head against his clavicle. His arm tightened about her waist, his cheek felt the softness of her hair, his hand the warmth of her skin radiating beneath her shirt, the shape of her hips and breasts pressing against him. He didn't know how long this might last before he caved in: no music played. This should have happened on the night of her prom—she'd been furious that he wouldn't take her, furious when he told her to do what every other respectable senior did, go with a date, that, yes, he'd arranged to be one of the prom's chaperones and, yes, he'd dance with her once, only once—and of course he couldn't dance with her then, he couldn't even permit himself to hold her for one dance at arm's length, for she wouldn't have allowed that, she would have closed the distance between them, and he'd refused to make a fool of himself in public when he'd never made a fool of himself during all those years, despite his private yearnings. They swayed slowly and held each other tightly, and he knew how dangerous the moment, this was a terrible mistake, it would take so little to forget where he ended and she began: and it took so little, one long deep kiss that might have become an everlasting trespass had Claire not finally pulled back, stopped moving her feet, freed her hands to hold his face and then quickly, sweetly, kiss him once again, then placed her fingers on his lips.

You're spoken for, Duncan, she whispered, you'll marry Meredith.

He felt his throat constrict, swallowed hard, nodded slightly.

And I'm giving you Iris's place as a wedding present. No— she said, placing the whole of her palm over his mouth—listen to me. Oldman has plans for June and Luke. When Sam returns, offer him this apartment. I don't want Iris's property. I won't sell it, and I won't use it.

She dropped her hand then, but not her gaze. He pulled her close, buried his face in her hair, inhaled her scent, and after a long moment loosened his grip and stepped back, let go. She turned away from him, crossed the room, picked up and put on her jacket, came back and emptied what was left in her glass into his, straightened. He took a deep breath, ventured: And if you had a reason to stay?

She smiled wryly, gently shook her head. Now that you've finally made good on your promise to dance with me, I don't even have a reason to return.

He followed when she stepped past him, but she raised a hand with her back to him, halting him in his tracks. She crossed the threshold, then turned to face him.

I love you, Duncan.

I know, he said. And then she was gone, her tread light on the stairs, the opening and closing of the door so quietly done that he wasn't sure until much later, when he'd finally summoned the courage to go downstairs, whether she'd left at all.

June

S H E   S T O O D on the cottage porch in the deep of night, the stars and moon lost, nowhere, not a glimmer of any universe beyond the blackness of the overcast shawling the sky. No light emanated from the upstairs of Iris's house to spill powdery shapes upon the garden: Claire was gone, had been for days, and Iris again sleeps in a pitch-black house. The cold air tangs of metal, June can taste the promise of snow. Her breath came from her in silvery wisps, and she willed her shoulders, arms, fingers to relax, go limp, willed the tension in her body to ebb, be gone, even as she watched Iris's house apprehensively. Iris, Claire told her before leaving, is dying, will soon die. June hadn't realized that, not fully—that *soon* shocked her—and now lives in daily fear that she, June, will be the one to find Iris dead. The thought that on any given morning, even tomorrow, Iris might not rise again sends a tremor that squirrels up her spine, the dead, as they say—no, perhaps in this case the near-dead—dancing on her grave. By the time she folds her arms and holds her elbows, the sensation is gone.

Claire was clear as to what June was to do when Iris dies: call Duncan, then go back to the cottage and keep Luke inside until he arrives. She told June this twice. Said as well: Arrangements have been made, you'll be taken care of.

Iris has repeatedly told Luke that she is going to hibernate this winter, like his turtle.

She has repeatedly told June: I am tired of dissolving.

June examined the incomprehensible sky. Without galaxy swath, without pinprick planet light, without the moon, nothingness stretched past infinity. She felt tired, crushed, hollow: the knowledge of Iris's certain death has left her reeling. The endless night, endless dark, mirrors her dismay. Iris's death-to-be has unmoored her: she knows she will not be able to bring herself to stay here, not be able to explain to Luke that Iris is gone. If she, they, remained, that empty house would not let him forget Iris; the day the garden turtle emerged into the spring's warmth Luke would expect Iris to do the same, to reappear: the child knows nothing of death, or of lies. June didn't know how to rail at the heavens, to rant aloud; instead, she lets the cold seep into her bones, stands within this barren season that remains sluggish, unborn, and under the heaviness of this dark that threatens to defy gravity, thwart the fall of snow, press upon Iris and suffocate her.

June already misses her. She feels oddly close to Iris; and but for Iris's sternness, her inviolable withdrawal from the world, they were not completely unalike. They never discussed their pasts or their private lives or voiced opinions; each was comfortable with the other's reticence; and if either communed with spirits or gods or prayed, each did so in the garden and did not let on. Iris came to love Luke, and June came to love Iris, not only because she took on the role of Luke's grandmother, but because she was nonjudgmental, reserved, committed to a way of life she'd created for herself, and stalwart in the face of her relentlessly devastating incapacities—the loss of coordination and strength, that slow slide into utter debilitation—never admitting to her needs in words, only in deed, allowing June to take over what Iris slowly, then more rapidly, became incapable of doing. If Iris's silence stemmed in part, in the beginning, from resentment, if June had indeed been an unwelcome guest—which she would never know for sure—she had never suspected.

Iris, *Iris,* June whispers. She summoned nothing by having spoken, not even the air stirred, words had no power over Iris's condition or the night's stillness. *Snow,* she begs heaven: Iris lives for the snow, lives to watch the day Luke will play in it, lives to see it cover the garden grounds, lace the trees' branches, cloak the cottage and leanto roofs. *Snow for Iris, for the little joy that is left to her, snow for me too,* June implored, *to stop these empty useless days and nights from pounding through me like blows.* She hasn't been able to bring herself to leave Iris alone during the days; at least if it snowed June would have an excuse to be in the garden, to shovel, to help Luke make a snowman, to momentarily remove herself from Iris, to momentarily push back that monstrous vastness—which June could not fathom or imagine filling—that awaits her. To momentarily forget Sam.

He told Luke that he'd be back, and he promised June the same. She doesn't know whether to believe him, or what his return might mean. They didn't speak of that, but they'd told each other what they dared. Sam: of the war, of how it changed him, of crazy Rita, of Freddie, of Leonard and the soup kitchen, of how Sam had come to the conclusion that he'd rather take the chance that a few thousand people might get used to him here than remain in the city, where seven or eight million people never would. And June: of the trailer park, of Auntie, of her walkabout mother, of the trip across the country, of the dog on the beach, of Ward. Of how she didn't know why Mabel, then Iris, had taken her in, or why Oldman — the kindest man in the world — had so generously made her and Luke a part of his life.

She misses Sam. She'd liked being with him, liked his quiet ways, liked the way he'd told her he didn't know whether to believe in lucky stars or guardian angels, but that before meeting Oldman his life hadn't had much rhyme or reason to it and that he'd felt for a long time that he was at its mercy, which hadn't been very merciful. She liked the way he'd said that if he ever took life by its tail, he'd have Oldman to thank; and that if he ever stopped letting things slip through his fingers, he'd probably have her to thank. She liked how gentle, how careful, he was with Luke. Liked that he'd asked her, shyly, what no one else ever had: Did you love him? — to which she replied, I wasn't allowed that. She liked the way they'd held hands with Luke, the child between them, and the way Sam sometimes pushed an errant strand of hair back behind her ears, smiled into her eyes. She liked that they hadn't kissed, that he hadn't pressed her, that he hadn't pretended they might have a future together; but now these things saddened her, leaving her to wonder — standing in that freeze beneath that empty sky — whether it saddened him too, whether she would ever know.

Ward had never said farewell.

And Iris would never, even if she knew beforehand the moment of her death.

Everyone, June was coming to realize, has their own way of bowing out.

Snow, she whispers, summoning the first flakes to fall on the palms of her open hands she raises toward the sky, *snow for us.*

Iris

THE FIRST SNOWFALL was light, but did not disappoint: it laced the boughs and fallen leaves and filled in the troughs of the furrows and the dimpled earth that had been turned over, sparkled on the leanto and cottage roofs. Where mounded, the soil poked dark veiny crests through the fragile whiteness. The snow did not melt, but on a day of dazzling sunlight softened, then froze in the night, leaving a crust whose shadows gleamed bluish and roseate.

The snow's appearance quickened Iris's spirit. She did not hibernate, indeed became more animated, more alert, sat awake through the days in that armchair that had been repositioned for her to face the garden. At times frost crystals made fantastic patterns in the window corners of the French doors. The boy's cold cheeks sometimes brushed against hers, the touch a capture of ice breeze. He always smelled of winter now, of its pure, frigid scent. The girl moved about as she always had, a phantomlike presence easy to mistake for nonbeing, and—without mentioning her delight, which Iris found apparent in the smoothness of June's expression, which no longer betrayed any disquiet—came to trust in what appeared to be a rally on Iris's part. Iris did not dissuade, simply dulled her tremors with larger doses of antispasmodics than she was allowed, and waited for what she imagined would be a perfect day, and marveled, for that thin snowfall had also blanketed her memories. She found herself living only in the moment and, when she reached back into the past, found herself rebounded, returned to the now and most recent present. She could summon at will the sound of Claire's movements on the upper floor, the pleasant sensation of Claire gently toweling her back, even more gently brushing Iris's hair, summon the intense gaze of those beautiful dark eyes, their final moments together, Claire saying *I'm glad I came,* and Iris demurring *And I'm glad you stayed.* She could, when alone, feel Luke resting in her lap, feel him reach up to twist a strand of her hair around his small fingers, smell the sweetness of his breath, feel his blood pulse beneath his wrist's thin skin, summon his laughter. She could see—and feel—the unspoken love June showered upon them both.

Iris was no longer dreaming of Matthew. By the second snowfall—which was so heavy that it bowed tree branches, bent bushes, buried all traces of the garden—she no longer dreamed at all. And she did not that day, or the next, or ever hibernate, and Luke didn't ask her if and when she would, for—delighted with the snow, excited by playing in it—he'd momentarily forgotten a turtle Iris did not recall, the one asleep in a small cave beneath a rock ledge that now couldn't be seen. Iris kept secret her discovery that, by combining doses of antispasmodics and sleeping pills, she could disengage from her body. She sat disengaged in that armchair and looked out upon the whitened garden's expanse littered with snow angel impressions, one small snow fort, and one darkly gleaming pathway shoveled from the leanto to the cottage to her own patio and then beyond to the outer door, and sometimes became mesmerized by the snowman—whose beatific smile and button eyes looked upon her kindly—that stood just beyond her patio.

All, Iris assured June, was as it should be. This, a perfect day: the low, unbroken overcast that presaged another snowfall to come before midnight; the boy who'd lain in her arms now frolicking in the snow with that unbridled joy only children and the innocent are capable of; the sandwiches made and wrapped and refrigerated, the tea served and cleared, the dishes done, everything in its place. The perfect day, and now the perfect dusk; the boy, racing along the shoveled path, made smaller by the waning light and, with that dark snowcap pulled low, as much like an elf as Claire had been at that age; the girl, waving at Iris, and then Luke rushing back to do the same. *Goodbye, goodbye:* and then they were gone, to Oldman's, and Iris—after the snowman and garden disappeared at day's end—put on the one floodlight that perched on the middle of the pergola's edge, and it illumined the snowman and beyond and, of course, made the dark in which she sat blacker than any night.

Perfect day, oh perfect night: yes, Iris decided again, all was as it should be. She'd thrown away the prescription vials during her daughter's visit, and no one knew how many pills Iris hadn't taken, how many she'd saved, how many she now fingered in a pant pocket, how many she would swallow: as many as there were, more than enough, she knew, to allow her what she had chosen as a perfect end to this perfect day, perfect night, and all that had come before. When June later that evening walked through the floodlit garden carrying her sleeping child, she never suspected that Iris still sat in the armchair, her gaze—upon the snowman—sightless, and her face serene.